MW00699443

Green ENVY

ALEATHA ROMIG

NEW YORK TIMES BESTSELLING AUTHOR

Book #2 of the SIN series

Aleatha Romig

New York Times, Wall Street Journal, and USA Today bestselling author of the Consequences series, Infidelity series, Sparrow trilogies: Web of Sin, Tangled Web, Web of Desire, and Dangerous Web, and the Devil's Series Duet

COPYRIGHT AND LICENSE INFORMATION

GREEN ENVY

resemblance to any actual persons, living or dead, events, or locales is entirely coincidental.

2021 Edition License

GREEN ENVY

SYNOPSIS

"Nothing is enough to the man for whom enough is too little." ~
Epicurus

At what age did I begin to question everything?

As far back as I, Donavan Sherman, can recall, I saw
the world not through the rose-colored glasses of others
—those spectacles worn by the individuals who see
what surrounds them and are satisfied—but through
vision hued by green.

Life took me along a bumpy path, or better yet, the
path I chose led me to encounter obstacles that
prepared me to overcome. That journey didn't sugarcoat
the world; it opened my eyes to the true qualities of
green—greed, illness, and envy. After all, even Disney
surrounds their villains in green smoke. That green hue
created the realization that there is always *more*, always
better, and *never enough*.

I saw, I coveted, I took, and I conquered.

I made enemies.

Even with Julia by my side, my quest for more isn't satisfied. There are people I want to see suffer, but it seems that revenge isn't a one-way street.

Will Julia pay the price for my sins?

From New York Times bestselling author Aleatha Romig comes a brand-new age-gap, family saga, chance meeting, contemporary romantic-suspense novel in the world of high finance, where success is sweet and revenge is sweeter.

Have you been Aleatha'd?

*GREEN ENVY is a full-length novel and book two of the Sin Series that began with RED SIN and will continue with GOLD LUST.

Julia

Back in the kitchen, I reached for the oven mitts and opened the top wall oven, removing the turkey breast. The second oven contained the casseroles to complete our holiday meal.

"What did Butler whisper before he left?" Van asked.

I shook my head. "It doesn't matter. Let's celebrate. My parents are gone and this is our first Christmas."

Van's smile returned. "The first item on that list definitely deserves celebration."

As I arranged the dishes, Van pulled a bottle of wine from the rack and brought down two glasses. My mind was on what Skylar had said.

I knew I shouldn't give Skylar or his ideas the time of day, but what he'd mentioned wasn't new. It was something I'd already wondered about. It was also the subject that Mrs. Mayhand had commented about, saying that some questions were better not asked.

Van handed me a glass of wine and lifted his own. "To our guests leaving."

A smile curled my lips as I stared at him, deep into his emerald eyes, and brought my glass to his. "To us being alone."

Our glasses clinked before we both took a sip.

A few minutes later before we were about to be seated, our food and wine already on the table, when Van reached for my hand. "I want to tell you every day that you amaze me because you do."

"I didn't make this meal."

"No," he said, the gold flecks in his orbs shimmering under the kitchen lights. "You did so much more. You stood up for yourself, and I couldn't be prouder."

He wrapped his arms around me, pulling me against his solid strength and to the place I wanted to be. Van had become that to me. He'd become my place of restoration, whether here in this big house, in the cabin, or in the wilderness. Within his presence, I felt at peace.

And yet there was a lingering question.

I looked up. "Van, who is Madison?"

The muscles of his torso tightened as his head tilted to the side. "Why are you asking?"

"Skylar said something. I don't want to believe him." I shook my head, still keeping my arms wrapped around

Van. "After all, I have all the reason in the world not to believe him. I believe you. Why is your company Sherman and Madison?"

He inhaled. "Once you go through all the information, you'll learn that Madison was a friend, and I chose to honor that friendship."

"Just a friend?"

Inhaling, he shook his head.

"I'm not asking as the writer," I said. "I'm asking as your fiancée. Who is Madison?" I said a silent prayer that Skylar had lied. After all, it couldn't be true. The pieces didn't fit.

Van's voice was deadpan as he answered, shattering our snow globe, "My wife."

Chapter 01

Julia

*V*an's hold of me continued as he awaited my response. We were two people in the eye of a hurricane with his answer swirling around us with category-five intensity, buzzing in my ears and muting the world beyond our shattered globe. The fire in the hearth a room away still snapped and crackled, the large clock on the wall still ticked, and yet all I heard was his response 'my wife' on repeat, the chorus within the melody of incessant buzzing.

I closed my eyes, lowering my chin and trying to make sense of what he'd said.

The buzz wasn't from Van's answer.

I heard it within me, the byproduct of my increased circulation racing through my veins. I was underwater and struggling to get to the surface, to make sense of what didn't make sense.

Staring up at the man still holding me, I took in his expression, longing for his lips to move, for him to explain what he'd said.

Still held against Van's wide chest, I sensed a new

tenseness in his stance. It was present in the way his arms tightened and the rigidity of his firm torso. I had a flashback of a story I'd read long ago where when a person gazed upon Medusa, they would turn from flesh and blood into stone.

With each passing second, Van closed himself down.

The image before me suddenly reminded me of the pictures I'd seen of him from a decade earlier. The sadness I perceived in those photographs was returning, materializing before my eyes. The man I knew, the one who saved me from the cold, fed me, and showed me what physical love was meant to be was slipping away, disappearing behind a mask that I didn't recognize.

His chiseled jaw clenched tight, and his lips pressed together, forming a straight line. Only his eyes spoke to me, talking to me in a way his words couldn't or wouldn't. They searched me, looking for understanding. The longer I stayed silent, the duller the emerald green became.

Taking a step back and bumping into the table, I broke free from his embrace.

Van reached out, seizing my arm. "Julia, you're not leaving."

My face snapped toward his.

Leave?

"I don't want to leave. That never occurred to me." I hesitated. "Is that what you think I'll do?"

Releasing me, Van took a step back and raked his hand over his handsome face. When his green orbs opened, a spark of light returned and yet he offered nothing more in the way of explanation.

My fingers grazed the edge of the table as the warm and appetizing aromas lingered around us. My focus went back to him. "I need more than what you said, Van. Tell me. Are you married? Is this" —I motioned around the large kitchen and to our uneaten meal— "all some kind of a joke, some grand plan to play me and my family? Are you ly...have you...?"

"No," he answered definitively as he stepped closer and reached for my hand. "This isn't anything like that. And I've never lied to you if that's what you're asking."

I was. I just couldn't make my mouth say the final word.

"I would never lie to you. That's why I told you the answer I did."

"That Madison is your wife, present tense?"

"No." He stood taller. "We never married, not legally."

"You proposed?"

He shook his head once. "No. I didn't lie to you about that either." He lifted my hand that he was holding and brushed his firm lips over my knuckles. "You, Julia McGrath, are the only woman to hear me say those words." A spark of light returned to his eyes. "And you are the only woman who has answered in the affirmative."

"I don't understand."

He exhaled. "I promise to explain it another time."

He tilted his chin toward the table. "Are we going to let Mrs. Mayhand's delicious holiday dinner go to waste?"

I couldn't ignore the ache in my chest. The place that only a short while ago was filled with hope and promise now had a void I wanted gone.

Who was this woman whom he named his company after?

Would she come in and irreparably shatter the snow globe I desperately wanted glued back together?

"Is Madison around?" I asked.

Van shook his head.

"Is she...passed...no longer alive?" When he didn't answer, I went on, "Van, I get it. I do. I would understand if you'd married before. After all, I saw the picture of you in your office, the one with you and the beautiful blond woman in a wedding dress."

"You didn't see what you thought you did."

"I know what I saw."

His head shook. "I wasn't married. I haven't. You will be the first Mrs. Donovan Sherman."

My eyes opened wide. "Oh my God. This is all about semantics. Tell me, was she Mrs. Donovan *Thomas?*"

Van smirked. "That could be a loophole. I'm fucking great at utilizing loopholes for all they're worth in business." He walked around me to my chair. "This isn't business, Julia. This is life and I'm telling you the answer as straightforward as I can." Pulling out the chair from the table, he motioned. "Sit. And do me the great honor of your presence without the ramifications of Butler's untimely misconception."

"Why can't you just answer?"

"I have." As I sat, he crouched down on his haunches before me. Reaching for my chin, his intense gaze stayed fixed on mine. "I will tell you what I can, and then I want to concentrate on you, not someone from my past."

I nodded as I twisted my legs and body toward him.

"Madison is still alive." His head shook and he shrugged his wide shoulders. "I believe. I haven't been told nor have I looked to learn otherwise. I haven't seen her in years, nor have we spoken. Whatever there was between us is over. It was over long before either of us knew."

"But the name of your company...?"

"I've done bad things, Julia." His expression contorted. "Bad things that I never regretted except where Madison was concerned. I suppose with the clarity of time and reason" —a smile curled his lips— "and because of the light you radiate by simply fucking being here, I now see that keeping Madison as part of my corporation's name was a reminder of what I'd done."

"Such as your last name?"

Van nodded; his Adam's apple bobbed. "Sherman is a reminder of what I'm capable of doing, that I'm capable of success while at the same time reveling in the defeat of others. Madison is different."

I leaned forward, placing my hand on his chest. The

steady beat of his heart confirmed this man was still flesh and blood. "Please tell me."

A shadow passed over him. "Madison is my way of punishing myself, a penance I pay each time I read or say her name." He ran his hands over my thighs. "Over time, the pain has dulled, but each time I succeed, her name reminds me that it's not enough. It's never enough."

"She's alive," I said softly as I framed his smooth cheeks in my hands. "I don't know which is worse, competing with a memory or a ghost."

His head shook. "Fuck, Julia, you're not in a competition. I'll have my legal team work on changing the name. It will simply be Sherman Corporation or perhaps" —he grinned— "Sherman and Julia."

"You'd do that?"

"If it would make you happy. That's all I want is for you to be happy."

I lowered my hands to my lap. "I don't want you to change the name. I want to know why you referred to her as your wife."

Silence settled over us as the delicious aromas filled the air, reminding my stomach that we hadn't eaten. Van took a deep breath before lowering his forehead to my thighs. When he looked up, it took every ounce of self-control not to fall to my knees and wrap him in my arms. Pain and regret emanated from his being so strongly that I felt it within me.

"There was a time," he said, "I pretended to be her

husband. It was for her own good. I wanted to get her the help she needed."

"Pretended?"

This time his hands came to my face, framing my cheeks. "Julia, I rarely ask for anything. If there's something I want, I take it. I'm asking for something from you right now."

"What?"

"I'm asking you to believe me and to put this conversation to rest. I'm asking to celebrate the holiday by giving me the greatest gift, that of trust."

Van was giving me an out, an exit. The neon sign was flashing, and I was ready to pass through. My motivation wasn't spurred by a lack of curiosity as to why Van referred to Madison as his wife. My reasoning was in front of me.

Right here, in the kitchen of Van's home, with a frozen world beyond the walls and windows, I not only saw but I felt Van's pain, literally, physically, as if dark tentacles were trying to wind and intertwine their sadness deep into my soul. I didn't want to spend any more of our time in their presence.

I forced a grin. "I thought I gave you your Christmas gift this morning."

The reminder of what I'd done—showing him how I found my own pleasure—what he'd asked me to do, returned a smile to his expression. Van's gaze lowered to where my thighs were held together and back to my eyes. "You did and watching you touch yourself was beautiful." He eased my knees apart and moved between them. "You're stunning. I guess I'm greedy because I want more."

My hands covered his upon my thighs. "You have my trust, Van."

"Do I?"

I pressed my lips together as I gave the question more thought.

He did.

Van's long fingers gripped my thighs through my slacks as his eyes pleaded. "Believe in me, Julia. Trust me. I've spent most of my life closed off, hiding who I am. I show the world one person, but that's not really me."

Thoughts of Van in his suit, in his mountain-man clothes, the man who chopped down a Christmas tree flashed through my mind.

He went on, "I've stayed closed off, alone, and in the dark."

"Van."

His head shook. "Closed off is fucking easier than being open with you, but damn it, I'm trying." He moved his hands, taking mine into his grasp. "You are light."

Squeezing my hands, he took a deep breath.

I couldn't look away from the kaleidoscope of emotions swirling in the green and gold of his eyes if I tried.

His volume rose. "The light, Julia. That is you.

Bright and beautiful. You're the damn sun. Do you know what happens when the sun rises?" He didn't let me answer. "It chases away the darkness. Your light will expose parts of me that haven't been seen in years, decades" —he shrugged— "or quite possibly—ever. I don't want to scare you, but I also won't lie to you. Some of what you'll learn and see won't be pretty. Some things I've done are downright grotesque."

His sincerity radiated in our touch. I heard it in his words and saw it in his expression. "I'm not scared."

"You should be." He took a deep breath, his chest inflating. "But know this, you won't be exposed to those things alone. I'll be with you, by your side forever." His grip of my hands tightened. "I won't let you go. You're mine. I found you." Lifting my hands, he brushed my palms with his lips, his kisses gentler than his grip. "What I'm asking of you is to be with me, trust me, and allow me the time to go slow, revealing the ugly truths most likely slower than you may want."

The lump forming in my throat grew bigger with each of his phrases. There were mysteries to this man, ones I would learn with time. However, it was the emotion I saw, heard, and felt that overwhelmed me. I was seeing Donovan Sherman exposed.

By the time he finished speaking, words failed me. I nodded as a lone tear slid down my cheek.

Van's arms pulled me close, tugging me from the chair into his embrace. Together, we fell onto the tile floor in a tangle of limbs until I was on my back, and he was over me. His handsome face was inches from mine, his arms supporting his torso above me while the length of his body and the hardness of his erection pressed between my legs.

Only our clothing stopped us from becoming one.

Brushing stray strands of my hair away from my face, Van asked, "Can you give me that?"

I nodded. "Trust and time."

"Yes." His chest vibrated as he let out a breath.

I grinned. "I don't need all the answers this minute —we have forever, right?"

"Forever."

His lips met mine as heat replaced the earlier anguish. Upon the hard kitchen floor, his hands roamed as his kiss deepened. Pulling apart from me, he asked, "Are you hungry?"

"I was, but now I'm hungry for something else."

Chapter 02

Julia

My questions about Van's past faded as lust and yearning filled the void. One by one, my articles of clothing disappeared until I was left fully exposed, completely vulnerable to Van's ministrations. The cold tile wasn't the only cause of the goose bumps peppering my flesh or the hardness of my nipples. He sat back on his heels, perched between my legs.

The earlier dullness in his orbs was gone. Van's gaze sizzled with the heat of his desire. "I need you to trust me."

"I do."

He offered me his hand. I stared for a minute, unsure why he'd stopped the foreplay. My core pulsated with unmet need as I laid my hand in his. As I stood, he led me back to my chair.

"I don't understand," I admitted.

His lips came to the sensitive skin of my neck and lower to my collarbone. "Sit and let me enjoy our meal and my gift."

His gift?

Time and trust.

Unsure of what Van had planned, I did as he said.

I licked my lips as he unbuckled his belt. Pulling it from the loops, he said, "Now give me your hands."

His deep voice rumbled through me as I sat naked upon the chair and offered him my hands. Van took each one and gently kissed each palm before directing me to place them behind me. He followed, out of my sight, behind the chair.

"What are you doing?"

My breath caught as Van began winding the soft leather of his belt around my wrists. My shoulders pulled as he secured my lower arms together. "Van?"

I'd never been bound.

As he continued his mission, the pull in my muscles stayed on the safe side of pain. My pulse kicked up as my breathing shallowed. Each tug was both frightening and erotic.

"Trust me." His timbre reverberated through me.

I did trust Van. I wanted to. Yet with each jerk of my arms, the unknown prickled my senses. I tried to squirm, but with the way my arms were now locked in place and my breasts pushed forward, I was left at his mercy. Warm breath teased my sensitive skin as he gently moved my long hair away from my breasts and to behind my shoulders, kissing and nipping my neck and lower to my collarbone.

Slowly, he moved around the chair, scanning me up and down. "Spread your legs. I want to see that beautiful, wet pink pussy."

"Van?"

He cupped my chin, pulling my gaze to his. "Are you wet?"

I nodded.

"Show me."

Each movement pulled on my arms, but with time, I was able to comply, opening my legs. Once I had, I again met his gaze. The sizzling I'd seen as he undressed me was now ablaze, an out-of-control wildfire radiating palpable heat.

"Van, tell me what you're going to do."

"Trust me."

He wasn't asking me a question, but if he were, I did trust him. It wasn't because I was without options—it was because I had given him my trust and he still had it. As I searched the depth of his stare, I voiced what I knew in my heart. "I do."

Van let out a breath. "Close your eyes and listen to my voice."

The baritone tenor settled over me as my eyelids obeyed.

I gasped as the chair was moved, turned to the side.

"Keep your eyes closed, Julia. Don't make me repeat myself."

A louder gasp filled the air as his large hands held

my thighs and his warm tongue ran the seam of my folds. Like a match to kindling, his mouth brought flames to my core, my insides twisted tighter as he licked and nipped. I longed to reach out, to weave my fingers through his dark mane, and pull him even closer.

Secured in place with my eyes shut, my other senses were on high alert as he shifted and his lips met mine. His kiss deepened as his tongue sought entrance.

"Taste yourself, Julia. You taste better than anything on this table."

I didn't back away as his lips again captured mine. When he pulled away, I was breathless as I waited for his next move. Everything inside me wanted me to look and watch this beautiful man as he did whatever he was about to do. However, he'd told me to keep my eyes closed, and for no other reason than to show him I trusted him, I wanted to comply.

"Open your lips."

The smooth edge of the wine glass came into contact with my lips as the tart and dry liquid covered my tongue. I hurried to swallow but not before wine dribbled down my chin and onto my breasts.

"Tsk-tsk," he murmured, his voice teeming with authority, causing my core to clench, "that won't do."

Before I could respond, his tongue lapped the wine from my skin. My nipples drew tighter as he purposely dribbled more of the wine over my breasts and down my stomach.

I stole a peek as he continued his torturous descent, licking and slurping while his touch moved even lower. My body was on fire as he pumped his long fingers inside me, his lips still sucking the liquid from my skin.

"Oh, Van."

I felt him move. The sounds of dishes and utensils filled my ears before his next command. "Open those sexy lips again."

The delicious scent of turkey and gravy preceded the bite of food landing upon my tongue.

"That's it. Swallow." After I complied, he said, "Open your eyes."

I wasn't sure when he'd done it, but my view was consumed with the lines on his toned abdomen, the definition of his arms, and the large erection before me. My lips curled into a grin as the sight of him caused me to momentarily forget that I was bound and helpless.

"Do you like what you see?"

"Very much."

"What do you want?"

"You mean besides you?" I asked.

"Yes, I plan on feeding you this dinner because you'll need nutrition for what I have planned next."

My eyes scanned the table. "Mashed potatoes."

"I was hoping you'd say that."

Van wasn't using the utensils as he dipped his fingers in the whipped potatoes. Melted butter dripped on my skin as he brought the bite to my lips. Without his prompting, I opened my mouth, taking in the delicious starch and licking his fingers clean.

Alternating between feeding me, feeding himself, offering me drinks of wine, and him drinking some too, Van proceeded to clean both of our plates and drain both of our glasses. With each bite and each sip, the wanton need within me grew. I'd never imagined that eating a holiday dinner could be so erotic.

"Tell me, Julia, have you had enough?" His chin tilted toward the stove and ovens. "I can get us more."

I shook my head. "I've had enough dinner."

"Oh," he said with a grin. "I forgot. Mrs. Mayhand also made us dessert."

"I want you for dessert."

He fell to his knees. "Me first."

Unlike earlier, there was nothing tentative or gentle in the way Van spread my legs and buried his face at my core. The prelude had me twisted with need. As his tongue lapped at my essence, my entire body shattered. I cried out as nerve endings detonated, a chain of explosions that went off from my head to my toes. I tugged against the belt to no avail as Van continued, through my orgasm and the next.

While my thoughts were flying high above the clouds, Van cleared away our plates, lifted my arms, and helped me from the chair. With my arms still bound, he turned me until I was facing the empty table. Pressure between my shoulder blades pushed me forward, my breasts pressing upon the hard, cool surface.

A soft kick to the inside of my ankles and my legs spread.

I called out as he held my hips and drove his full length deep into my core. My cheek slid over the smooth table. Without my hands, I was unable to find a grip as he pounded into me. The gentleness he'd exercised while feeding me was gone. Contrary to his actions, his tenor was deep and soothing as the air filled with words of praise and devotion.

Although I wasn't sure it was possible since I'd already come more than once, before I could prepare, I was overcome with a world-shattering orgasm. As my core spasmed, hugging him, Van continued his thrusts. Faster and faster. My hips bounced against the table's edge. The weight of his body held me in place while pushing on my bound arms. Every nerve was electrified as pain was forgotten, washed away by overwhelming pleasure.

Thrust after thrust, Van continued taking what I'd already offered.

He was an animal consumed with the task at hand and yet he also tended to my needs, his fingers teasing, swirling, and pinching my clit, his kisses and nips raining over my neck back, and shoulders. His attention to my breasts came when he'd lessen his weight, allowing himself access.

I wanted nothing more than to turn, to wrap my arms around his neck, and continue this dance, this primitive ritual that had started with the first man and woman. The frustration as I pulled against the belt would come only to be washed away by another orgasm. Nothing slowed his pursuit. Faster still, he pounded until finally he stilled. His fingers dug into my hips, his cock throbbed, and his deep growl reverberated through the kitchen as his seed filled me to overflowing.

Sandwiched between Van's solid frame and the table as my arms and shoulders ached and my core was satisfied and filled, the realization hit. This odd and unusual combination of pleasure and pain had consumed me in the best of ways. As Van pulled out of me and gently unwrapped his belt from my arms, my thoughts were consumed by what we'd done, what he'd done.

He'd annihilated my concerns and centered my entire focus on the pleasure that only he could provide.

My arms fell lifeless to my sides as exhaustion prevailed. I continued to rest upon the table's surface. Gently Van turned me, lifting me to my feet and into his arms, raining kisses over my cheeks until my eyelids rose, and our gazes met. "You were perfect."

"I think it was all you. I was, as they say, tied up."

His grin grew as he ran his finger over my cheek. "Do you regret trusting me?"

The void that I'd felt earlier in my chest was gone. Beyond the windows, the dark sky was littered with light flurries dancing within the illumination of the outside lights. Taking all my energy, I lifted my arms to Van's shoulders and pushed myself up on my toes until our lips touched. "I don't regret it." My forehead fell to his chest. "Thank you," I mumbled against his warm skin.

"For what?"

"For fixing our snow globe."

Van
Over Twenty Years Ago

My mind was too consumed with all that was happening, all the balls in the air. My drive to succeed, to accomplish more, to show the world I was capable ruled my thoughts and physical being. When the time came to sleep, I'd lie down only to stare at the ceiling. It was as if my body couldn't rest, knowing that there were i's to dot and t's to cross. There were people to schmooze and investments to be made.

And then there was the fucking tightrope—the balancing act of stretching assets until they were so taut, they were ready to snap. It was no secret: I wasn't working with a large budget. That also didn't impede my determination that one day I'd have more.

More money—more power.

I was on the verge of greatness. It was right there, close enough to touch.

It would happen.

That belief wasn't conceit. It was that deep-down-fucking-to-your-toes knowledge that I was meant for more than some small-town schmuck from Texas. Chicago was my new home, the third-largest city in the country, and the place where I would become more.

It was where I came to reinvent myself.

Lost in the cloud of thoughts, I barely saw outside my own bubble. My inability to sleep had me up in the middle of the night at a nearby coffee shop. Stepping inside, I gazed around the nearly empty café, my focus momentarily attracted to a woman.

There was something about her that caught my eye.

Nothing in my life had me interested in developing a relationship. There already wasn't enough of me to go around. And yet I was drawn to her, the way she sat contentedly alone, in the middle of the night, consumed with her task at hand. With her light-yellow hair as a veil hanging over her face, a paper cup of coffee on the table, she was staring down at a book.

Is she like me, with too many fires lit to sleep?

While I was intrigued, my mind wasn't fully on a woman.

My thoughts were racing with my latest project. My start-up company was gaining investors. The concept was simple. Only a year earlier the world had survived the predicted Y2K collapse of technology.

It seemed that these days everyone was working to navigate the worldwide web. At the same time, they were willingly divulging their personal information. SixDegrees was a relatively new way to connect to friends and family. Only in its infancy, the platform had potential. It was also a place to share, something the average person was all too willing to do.

My start-up was an investment in a programming idea. These programs created firewalls, obstacles to people's protected personal information. Whether gaming or creating an account on SixDegrees, people entered their names, addresses, sometimes their Social Security numbers. The information was requested for demographic data. And it was a ticking time bomb.

The worldwide web was growing, and I predicted that in time, it would only grow more. The world was shrinking, and the web was the next step in communications.

I foresaw a future when anything we wanted to know would be at our fingertips, eliminating the need to spend countless hours and days thumbing through old periodicals or obsolete textbooks.

The web was also facilitating communication as revolutionary as the invention of the telephone. Telecom companies were struggling to keep up. Every family wanted their own computer. Though home computers became available in the early 1980s, twenty years later, the desire had multiplied exponentially. This technology was the way of the future and only had one way to go.

More.

Bigger.

More powerful.

Working my way through college, I saw the potential of investing in web-based companies.

What could be better?

Create web-based products, ones that would be wanted by the masses.

The old way of creating items that lasted forever was disappearing for a reason. The idea of the refrigerator in my parents' home that was as old as we children didn't provide incentive for buying new. The world was changing. The technology was moving at unprecedented speed. I knew that I wasn't the only one who wanted the best and the top of the line.

My theory was to capitalize on the individual's need for more, their lack of satisfaction. Release a program and within months, release a better one. And six months later, better than that. It was a spiral that would spin over the world—a tornado to demolish what was old, leaving behind the innate need for new.

Taking my cup of coffee, I made my way to the long bench with small two-person tables, sitting a few feet away from the blond. Facing her direction across our tables, I waited. It was as she looked up and I saw her staggering green stare that I grinned. "It's late to be out alone."

"If that's a threat, I know the owner."

My laugh came from my chest.

How long has it been since I'd laughed?

"If I wanted to threaten you, I wouldn't do it in a

shop lit up like midday. I'd wait until we were alone in the parking lot."

The woman's forehead furrowed. "You've given this some thought."

"I hadn't. Now I am."

She lifted a small cellular phone from her open purse. "I could call the police."

"You could. Is it illegal to have conversation with a beautiful woman?"

She laid the phone on the table near her book.

"What are you reading?" I asked.

She lifted a dog-eared paperback. "*The Canterbury Tales*."

"Geoffrey Chaucer."

"I'm impressed."

My smile grew. "So am I."

"Have you read?"

"I read." I took a sip of my coffee. "Yeah, it was required."

She nodded. "That's why I'm reading it too. It's the old English that's taken me time to get used to."

"It's poetic in a way."

"As an art major, I'd rather paint than read."

I nodded. "Think of Chaucer's verse as art using a different medium, that of words." I gave the collection more thought. "I found the depiction of different social classes fascinating. I liked how he used the pilgrimage to bring together various people from different walks of life. That separation of classes still exists."

A cloud seemed to pass over her expression. "Yeah, I know."

It was the cloud even more than her smile that intrigued me.

Why is this woman sad in a coffee shop at this hour?

She took a deep breath. "I'm Madison, Madison Montgomery."

"Hello, Madison Montgomery. My name is Donovan. Friends call me Van."

"I'm not really a friend."

"Not yet."

Chapter 04

Van
Present Day

The office building was quiet at this early hour, the day after Christmas. Technically, since the twenty-fifth landed on a Sunday, today was the observed holiday. The employees of Sherman and Madison had the day off to continue their celebrations. A smile ghosted across my expression as I recalled Julia's and my celebration.

Last evening, for a few moments, I'd been concerned that my answer regarding Madison had ruined everything. There was a time when I'd wanted Madison to have the title of wife. I'd wanted it enough to decimate the entire world if it would lead her to me. My obsession with her was unhealthy. That was what some PhD in some book said. I probably could have benefitted from actual therapy.

Men like me don't confide their secrets to anyone, not even someone with the promise of doctor-patient confidentiality. Nothing was completely secure.

Everyone had a price or at the very least the possibility of being hacked.

The only person who knew what lurked in the recesses of my mind and memories was the same person who had shared her secrets. We both knew our confidences were safe with one another because if they weren't, all would be revealed. Lena had been on my mind since our last call. For once, I hadn't been fully honest. I hadn't been ready to share Julia, not yet.

Hanging my wool topcoat and my suit jacket on the hall tree in the corner, I shut the door to my private office and walked to the windows. I'd seen the movies and read the books. A man like me stereotypically had floor-to-ceiling windows with an expansive view of a cityscape. Tall buildings would have their spires stories below where I stood, making my building the tallest in the skyline.

That wasn't me.

I didn't need an ostentatious air to compensate for anything.

A tall building wasn't necessary to offset a small dick.

A grandiose view was truly in the eye of the beholder.

I had a corner office. I peered beyond the windows from the third story of a hundred-year-old building. In one direction, I saw the view that beckoned me to Ashland, the Chequamegon Bay. From the other windows,

I looked out over the small city. There weren't towers reaching into the sky nor were there buildings branded with my name or the name of others in bright lights.

The quaintness of this area had been my refuge.

A big fish in a little pond, some would say.

That wasn't true anymore.

My pond was connected to all the other ponds, streams, rivers, lakes, and oceans. Much the way Ashland, Wisconsin, was built on the mining of ore and the ability to transport it through the waterways, today's world was connected.

It wasn't through the waterways but via technology.

Recognizing the magnitude of the web propelled my success. It was the foundation that allowed for bigger and better ventures.

Popping a K-cup in the coffee maker, I hit the start button and made my way over to my desk. Gently moving the mouse, my three screens came to life. After entering my password, my first task was to look for Connie's email. Despite this being her day off, she knew I would be here, following up on the list of issues she'd brought to my attention yesterday, not limited to the messages from Phillip Thomas.

My jaw tightened at the sheer absurdity of his call. It was more than that. Shutting the door on family meant the damn door was closed in both directions. After a fucking decade, if Phillip thought I gave a rat's ass about his opinion, he had a higher opinion of himself than he deserved.

My attention went to my emails as I clicked one purely out of curiosity at the person who sent it. "Well, let's see what you have to say, Marlin."

The coffee maker stopped spitting and spurting, signaling that my coffee was ready. I went for my warm mug and settled back in my leather chair. Focusing on the email, I began to read.

Sherman,

Interesting to learn of your interest in Wade Pharmaceutical. Your recent acquisitions have made you a formidable shareholder. Skylar informed me of your interest in our trials as well as your offer to acquire the shares held by the Butler family.

If you are serious about either or both inquiries, the conversation should not occur in written form. Come to Chicago, look me in the eye.

Until then, nothing will be shared.

M. Butler

Taking a sip of the hot coffee, I scoffed at his false bravado. Marlin Butler knew I had him beat. The most shares he could possibly acquire would be the ten remaining shares held by four or five different entities. That was the most, but he wouldn't get them. I clicked on an email from Jeremy, Lena's guru.

Jeremy didn't disappoint. He had the answer I sought.

The remaining ten shares of Wade Pharmaceutical were owned by three entities. I was certain it was more.

Is someone else accumulating stock?

I stared at the names of the corporations listed as shareholders. One name, the owner of five percent caught my attention—Aphrodite Corporation.

Setting the coffee mug down, I shook my head and began searching, wondering if Jeremy knew the person behind that corporation.

How can he not?

If he does, why would he tell me?

My message was short.

Why tell me about Aphrodite?

I hit send.

The return message came quicker than I anticipated.

She wanted you to know.

Fuck.

I looked up the other two entities: GreenSphere Opportunities and Wolfe Acquisition Limited. They were both Special Purpose Acquisition Companies.

SPACs are relatively new. Their purpose was to raise money in anticipation of buying private companies, basically taking them public without the traditional public offering.

Why are large SPACs interested in Wade Pharmaceutical?

It made less sense than my interest. There was only one possibility. Someone had leaked the information about Wade's possibility of an Alzheimer drug.

My next call was to Aphrodite.

The call only rang twice.

"Donavan, it's a holiday." Lena's tone was sweet like hard Christmas candy—sweet yet capable of destroying from the inside out.

"I received Jeremy's email."

"And imagine that, his email accomplished what took me numerous calls only a week ago to do."

Lena was Aphrodite—the ancient Greek goddess of sexual love and beauty. We'd laughed when she originally set up the LLC.

"Sell me your five percent," I said.

"Oh, I thought it would be fun to be back in business together." Lena laughed. "I began to think about our conversation last week. You know, I also want to see the Butlers go down. And I simply detest being on the outside looking in."

"What do you know about GreenSphere and Wolfe?"

"I know that right after I acquired the shares, GreenSphere offered me an investment opportunity.

Whoever they are, they want in something fierce. Their offer was almost too good to pass up."

Why haven't they contacted me?

"And you don't know who they are?" I asked.

"You want a lot of answers for a man who still hasn't told his best friend the real reason for his interest in Wade Pharmaceutical."

"You saw the press release." The press release announcing Julia's and my engagement.

Lena hummed. "Not the way I'd expect to hear that my partner in crime is engaged. Did you forget about the engagement the last time we spoke?"

Leaning back against the soft chair, I ran my free hand over my face. "You wouldn't get it."

"Try me."

I'd been open with Julia. As I prepared to speak to Lena, I wondered if last night had opened some sort of dam. The difference was that Lena knew my past, all of it. She was wanting my present. "Julia is different."

"Go on," she encouraged.

I stood, sending my chair backward against the wall. "Fuck, Lena, I'll say it. I love her."

"Excuse me, put Donovan Sherman back on the phone."

Standing at the window, I didn't see the frozen bay but a slide show of the memories I'd accumulated over the last week and a half.

How is it possible that Julia has affected me this strongly in such a short time?

"My interest in Wade is to keep it going and make it more for Julia."

"Oh goodness. This is simply spine-tingling. Why wouldn't I want to be a part of that?"

In hopes of repairing our bond, I offered more details. "Butler is fucking Julia's parents, their company, and their future. If I didn't hate the man—fuck, the whole family—before, I would now. But as you know, I already hate them."

Lena's tone softened and her volume lowered. "You're hosting my kind of party, Van. I'm always down for revenge and crude sex. I assume your fiancée is into kink or you wouldn't chain yourself to her for the rest of your life."

I had no intention of discussing Julia's and my sex life. "Sell me your shares."

"No. Introduce me to your new woman."

There was a primal and visceral reaction in hearing that description—*my* woman.

"Would she be open to a three-way?" Lena asked. "I mean, as long as it's not past her bedtime."

I gritted my teeth. "Sell me your shares."

"Logan called."

The change of subject caused the small hairs on the back of my neck to rise. "You? Logan Butler called you and you answered?"

"He's doing his brother's bidding. He asked about you and wanted a way to reach you."

"I'm not hiding. I received an email from Marlin today."

"That's interesting but not as interesting as the tidbit Logan let drop during our conversation."

I held the phone tighter. "You have my attention."

"Before Logan called me, it seems that he had a nice, long conversation with Phillip."

"Fuck," I mumbled under my breath. "Is that why Phillip has been harassing Connie?"

"Your brother is basically broke, in more than the sense of finances," Lena said. "You knew that. You're the reason for most of his woes."

"He made his own decisions."

"Desperate people do desperate things."

"What does that mean, specifically regarding Logan and Phillip?"

"It means they've found a common goal."

"Fucking with me," I said. "That's hardly new."

"Introduce me to your child bride-to-be, Van. She's going to need a female friend who understands the dangers lurking in the shadows now that she's associated with you." Before I could respond, she added, "Let's say she can think of me as her big sister."

Lena had a little sister. It wasn't Julia.

Because you did such a great job with your own sister...I wouldn't say that either. Lena was hardly the singular reason for what happened. She'd tried. I shook my head.

"Julia's safe from shadows," I said, "or anything or anyone else. I'd fucking protect her with my life."

Lena's cadence slowed. "And *they* know that."

"Sell me your shares, and I'll work out a way to introduce you." Not that I'm letting you alone with Julia. I didn't add the last part. The truth was I admired Lena more than almost anyone. That said, I didn't trust her any more than she trusted me.

"Are you really going there, Van, tit for tat? I'm not selling. Those shares are my credit, my stepping-stone. After all, the interest Donovan Sherman has taken in Wade has thrust it into the spotlight. Let me in on this. I'll work GreenSphere. Butler won't sell to you, but he might to Aphrodite or GreenSphere. You and I invest in GreenSphere and those shares fall under their umbrella. It will be almost like they're ours. Then when Wade makes its Alzheimer research known, we can hold hands, sing Kumbaya, and watch as Wade's value soars and the Butlers are left in the cold."

"How the fuck did you know about the Alzheimer research?"

"The compound that Wade has kept quiet? Like I said, Logan and I chatted. Let me join the fun, Van."

There was no better partner if our goals remained the same.

The problem was that there was also no more capable opponent than Lena Montgomery if our goals changed.

Chapter 05

Julia

Sitting in the library with the fire roaring in the fireplace and surrounded by Donovan's life as reported by others, I was lost down a rabbit hole of his business endeavors dating back to about fifteen years earlier. In what I was reading, the acquisition of Sherman Brothers Department stores was still fresh and raw. From what I read, it appeared as though Donovan was drowning in lawsuits that claimed everything from improper business practice to the theft of the employees' retirement savings.

I'd heard this story directly from Van but reading through it in chronological order was nerve-racking. If it were a book, I might skip to the last page to make sure Van succeeded. I didn't need to flip to the end. I was sitting in his opulent home on his large estate and knew that he hadn't been taken down by the litigious attacks or the bad press.

There was a lot of bad press.

Submersed in those thoughts, I jumped at the chime of the doorbell.

That's what I assumed it was. In all the time I'd been here, no one had ever come to the door except for my family, and they were expected. Laying the article upon the stack with others, I stood. As I made my way to the front door a sense of trepidation came over me.

Who would come to Donovan's home?

I was halfway to the door when the chimes rang again and at the same time my phone buzzed in the pocket of my soft pants. Pulling out the phone, I saw Van's name.

Instead of saying hi, I jumped to the matter at hand. "Someone's at your door."

"*Our* door," he corrected. "I meant to call you sooner. It's Margaret. She picked up a few things and asked if she could bring them by today."

I exhaled in relief. "I was afraid it was my parents again."

"I'll be home soon."

"Really?" I asked. "It's only two in the afternoon."

"Everything is still closed because of the holiday. I'll explain when I get home."

I was now to the doors to the entryway. "Okay, see you soon."

"Julia..."

I waved to Margaret through the sidelight. "I'm letting Margaret in. What is it?"

Van seemed to hesitate before he said, "You're the best fucking thing I've ever done. I just wanted you to know that."

His words made me smile, filling my cheeks with warmth. As I reached for the doorknob, I saw the marks his belt left on my wrists and pulled the sleeve of my sweater lower to my hand. The marks from the belt weren't my only souvenirs of last night. My hips bore marks from the edge of the kitchen table.

"Hi," I said, opening the door wide as momentarily frigid air swirled around us. "Goodness. Come inside."

Margaret's arms were filled with shopping bags. It wasn't food she was delivering but bags with names on the outside I recognized—Saks, Nordstrom, Neiman Marcus, Bloomingdale's, Henri Bendel. Those were the ones I read as Margaret kicked off her boots and carried the bags into the living room.

"Merry Christmas," she said with a grin. "I hope you like everything, but if you don't, I can return it."

Although this was only our second meeting, I took a moment to look at Margaret, not as someone who works for Van but at *her*. She was probably younger than my parents and older than I. There was a genuine sweetness to her smile that drew me in and made me feel as if she didn't judge me.

I lifted one of the bags. "Is there a Saks Fifth Avenue in Ashland that I missed?"

"No, but we have some great boutiques. Donovan asked me to order these things online." She lifted one bag as the blush in her cheeks deepened. "If I hadn't realized you weren't Olivia before, this little bag of lingerie would have been a good hint."

"Olivia?"

"Donovan's sister." Her eyebrows danced as she held the bag.

Taking it from her, I peered inside. Each item was wrapped in tissue paper. The first one was a pair of lace panties. "Oh. I guess this was a good clue." Warmth crawled from my chest to my neck. "How did you know my size?"

"I guessed. Again, everything can be returned."

I motioned toward the living room. "Would you like to stay?"

She looked around the large open space and connecting rooms. "It's odd to be here and not be cleaning."

"I could get us some tea or coffee to warm us up. It gets a little lonely here during the days."

Margaret pulled the scarf from around her neck and pushed her gloves into the pocket of her coat. "Thank you. I'd welcome the break."

My eyes opened wide. "Oh, I just remembered that today is still the holiday. I don't want to intrude on your time more than I have."

"You haven't. This was a fun task."

I gestured to the collection of bags. "How did you get all of this today?"

"Some came in on Saturday. The rest came today. Apparently, if you pay enough for shipping, even the holidays won't stand in the way of delivery."

I shook my head. "Donovan shouldn't have. I have clothes."

Margaret's eyebrows danced again. "For a man, he has very good taste. I wouldn't be hard on him if I were you."

"Now I'm anxious to see what you brought."

Margaret laid her coat on one of the chairs. "I could get the coffee if you want to look."

"How about I help with the coffee, and we can look together?" I hesitated. "Unless the contents will make me blush."

"Some might, but I've seen them, so if you blush it will be because you're imagining showing them to someone else."

I grinned. "The someone who picked them out and sent you on a shopping spree."

"That would be him."

"I think he wanted the reassurance that they were items a woman would like."

Once in the kitchen, instead of using the big coffee pot, I read the different flavors aloud and added the appropriate pods to the coffee maker. "Thank you for bringing all of that here on a holiday and in the cold."

"The cold isn't going away anytime soon. Besides, my son is busy playing the new video games he received for Christmas. My husband is in his workshop where he'll be for hours." She exhaled. "This is nice."

I handed her the mug with the hot, vanilla-flavored coffee. "It is."

We both sipped our coffee before Margaret sighed. "Julia, if you don't mind me saying, I'm glad you're here."

"You are? I wasn't sure what you or Paula thought about my presence."

"There are conflicting stories about Donovan around these parts—probably everywhere."

I nodded. "I was just reading some stories from years ago. Van told me the story, but the news coverage was brutal."

Margaret sighed. "It's as they say about it all the time. You can't believe everything you read or hear."

"I think that's why Van originally wanted his memoir written. He wants the truth out."

"The truth or his truth?" She shook her head. "Regardless, he deserves to tell his side." She took another drink. "Mr. Sherman is more than what others say about him. He's been incredibly good to our family. Over the years, he's stayed rather isolated. I've always wondered if he was lonely. This is a big house."

"It is," I agreed.

"You don't need to worry," she said with a smile. "As far as Mom and I are concerned, you have a cheering section."

My smile grew. "I like that."

"We want him to be happy."

I nodded. "Me too. Do you want to help me look in all of the bags?"

"If you want me to."

Together we carried the numerous bags upstairs and toward my suite. It was as we approached the door that I remembered I'd forgotten to make the bed. That wasn't completely accurate. I rarely made the bed. "The suite may be a bit messy."

Avoiding the back bedroom, we stayed in the front sitting area, both sitting on the couch, the bags at our feet. As I picked up the first one, Margaret stopped me.

"I appreciate the invitation, I do. However, now that we're here, I think Donovan should be with you when you do this. After all, he did pick the items out."

"Don't let me interrupt."

We both turned toward the deep voice coming from the open door. Filling the space, wearing his custom suit and looking like he'd stepped off the cover of GQ, Van's smile was absolutely panty-melting as he eyed me surrounded by all the bags.

"You said no gifts," I said with a grin.

"Margaret," Van began, "did you explain that these aren't gifts?"

"They aren't?" I asked before she could respond.

"No," he said. "They're on loan. If you like them, then we can work out something."

"Something like what?"

He came closer. "I'm always up for negotiation. I'm sure we can come up with some sort of trade. Let the bartering begin."

"And that's my cue." Margaret stood and smiled our

direction. "You know what? I just remembered this thing I needed to do."

"You don't need to go," I said. "And if you do, you're welcome back."

Margaret nodded. "We're cheering, Julia. Remember that. It's nice to see you, Mr. Sherman."

Van nodded. "I can't thank you enough for always coming through."

"My pleasure."

"Thank you again. I can show you out," I offered.

"I know the way," she said with a grin as she passed through the doorway. "Enjoy the non-gifts."

Van reached for my hand, encouraging me to stand. We both remained silent as we listened for the sounds of Margaret's departure. Finally, he spoke, "I didn't mean to spoil your ladies' time."

"You didn't, but...it was nice."

He nodded. "I forget that you're here alone all day. I know you are." He ran his finger over my cheek. "I have a long way to go, Julia. Speak up. Tell me what you want or what's missing."

I looked down at all the bags. "I doubt anything is missing."

His expression sobered as he gently pushed the sleeve of my sweater upward, revealing the marks left behind by his belt. "Fuck."

"It's not as bad as it looks." Warmth filled my cheeks. "I read online that satin is the most forgiving."

Van's eyes widened. "You researched bondage online?"

"I mean, I didn't use that word. I don't want those cookies."

He wrapped his arms around me and pulled me close. "I didn't mean to hurt you."

"You didn't. I probably fought it more than I should have."

"Don't do that."

I peered up at him. "Do what?"

"Minimize or make excuses for my behavior." He lifted one of the sleeves, studying the markings. "This was too much. I..." His nostrils flared as his gaze came back to mine. "You are precious, delicate, and special. I went too far, desperate for your trust."

"You have it, Van. I'm not complaining. I didn't hate it."

He scoffed. "That's a rousing review."

My hands went to his shoulders as I stood on my tiptoes and brushed my lips against his. "I liked it. I've never—"

"Another first."

He reached for my hand and gently ran his fingers over my lower arms. When his gaze met mine, his words were laced with his remorse. "I'm sorry. The hickey, I meant those. I like you wearing my mark, but not like this."

"We can try satin," I said with a grin. "The idea isn't a no-go for me."

His forehead met mine. "Julia, you're so strong. I can't believe I found you."

"I'm glad you did." As I spoke, I noticed the daylight out the window, realizing the time. "Why did you say you were home early?"

"I realized I'd rather be here with you."

My smile grew. "I'm glad you're here." We both looked at all the bags. "Now I'd like to see what you chose for me. Margaret says you have good taste."

"She's giving me undue credit. Let's see what she purchased or maybe you could give me a fashion show, model each item."

"I saw the lace panties. If I model item by item, we'll be at this until late at night."

Van reached for my hand. "Before we get lost in the sexiness of you, with or without clothes, I wanted to let you know that I spoke with my banker and your father. I'm paying Wade Pharmaceutical's balloon payment first thing tomorrow morning when the banks open. I'm also going to need to travel to Chicago for some logistical PR. I figured you could come with me and gather some of your things to bring back here."

I shook my head. "You're making the balloon payment and you want to go to Chicago? I-I don't want to go back until after the date of my wedding, my *not* wedding... you know?"

"I'm afraid the business at hand won't wait."

I took a step back as a twinge of unease prickled my skin. "I don't feel right about any of this. How much was the payment? Are you writing up something so that it will be repaid? Did your legal team? What about Wade's legal team?"

"I have the documents on the computer. I'll be happy to share them with you later."

"How much?" I asked again.

"I want to tell you not to worry about it."

"But you won't because you've encouraged me to be active in the running and operations of Wade."

Van took a deep breath. "Three quarters of a million. An equal payment will come due in another sixty days if the lending institution isn't satisfied with the profit-and-loss figures between now and then."

I pulled away and paced to the windows and back. "No. First, I think we should stay here in our globe. And second, I was wrong to ask you to make that payment. My dad can find—"

Van seized my hand and brought me to a stop. "I've spoken with him. This is what's best. My interest in Wade and pharmaceuticals in general has stirred up a few unexpected consequences. Right now, the main goal is to increase spending on the research for the new medication. Approvals take time, but first the CDC needs the data. Without trials there won't be approval."

My forehead fell to his chest. "I spent the day learning about you, working on things for your memoir, and I should be doing what I can for Wade."

"Hey," he said, lifting my chin, "you researched safe

bondage techniques. That alone is worth what I'm spending on that payment."

"How can I ever thank you or repay you?"

"We're partners, Julia. Once we're married, your parents' shares will divert to you. Come with me to Chicago and address the board of directors. Take your rightful place."

I inhaled, thinking about his words and wondering how I felt about doing as he said. Before I could come up with a reply, Van went on.

"I have twenty-six percent of the shares with the potential of more, although that's looking less likely."

"Why?"

Van shook his head. "I never lied to you. I promised I'd do what I could and I am. I wanted you to know that." His smile grew. "Now let me watch the woman I love open these bags."

Tears came to my eyes. "You *love*?"

"If you can't tell that, you're not paying attention, or I've done a shitty job showing it."

I shook my head. "I-I think I love you too. I was reading about you and all that happened after the takeover and dissolution of Sherman Brothers."

"If corporate intrigue increases your affection level, I promise there's a lot more."

My cheeks rose. "No, it's not the intrigue; I found myself worried that you wouldn't survive the court battles. I realized I cared. You're not some person in multiple articles, you're you." I laid my palm on his chest. "You're the man I trust and—it may be too soon but—the man I love."

"Who said love has a timetable? Don't they talk about love at first sight?"

"I think most people would agree that particular emotion is more accurately defined as lust."

Van's fingers splayed on my back beneath the soft sweater. "Oh, I have that too." His large hand came down with a slap on my covered ass. "Now, let's look in some bags. Maybe we'll find something for you to wear when you meet with Wade Pharmaceutical's board of directors."

My stomach twisted at the thought.

"Not the lace panties," I said, hoping to lighten my mood.

"Not that they can see," Van clarified.

Chapter 06

Julia

*E*arly Wednesday morning before the sun rose, Van and I arrived at a small private airport outside of Ashland. As Van parked his truck and I waited on the tarmac, I was struck with the insignia painted on the side of the Cessna.

Sherman and Madison appeared in large letters that from my vantage point, seemed to be at least six feet tall.

Despite the long wool coat covering my slacks and blouse, lined leather gloves, and boots, a chill ran through me. The sensation wasn't associated with the sub-zero temperature or the wind swirling and blowing loose strands of hair around my face but from something within.

Around me, the small airport hummed with activity as sparse flurries danced in the beams of the tall lights. Workers called out to one another as other planes were tugged by small tractor-like contraptions from their hangars. Moments ago, I saw a person inside the plane with Van's company's name. The steps were down, giving me a view into the fuselage. The open door could be interpreted as a greeting and still I hesitated, my boots staying on the concrete as I remained momentarily transfixed by the insignia.

My face tilted, taking in the swirled letters. With each sighting of the name, I longed to learn more, wished that I didn't care, and at the same time, feared what may come to light.

Van's footsteps clipped along the tarmac seconds before he reached out, placing his gloved hand in the small of my back. The layers of clothing and outer garments muted the warmth of his touch, its presence only revealed in the pressure he applied.

"Why aren't you in the plane?" he asked as he led me toward the steps.

Blinking away my focus on the words, I feigned a smile. "I was waiting for you. I don't know anyone on the crew, and they don't know me."

Van pulled me close, his height and breadth protecting me from the cold wind as the shower-fresh scent surrounding him teased my senses.

"Stop worrying about Chicago," he said before gesturing for me to lead as we ascended the small stairs.

I wanted to tell him that it wasn't Chicago that was on my mind, but before I could utter the words, we were greeted by an older man in a pilot's uniform.

"Mr. Sherman," the man said with a nod of his head. Small lines formed around his eyes as he smiled, and gray peppered his otherwise-dark hair.

"Andrew," Van began, "this is my fiancée, Julia McGrath. I'm sure you'll be seeing more of her." Van's smile shone down at me. "Julia, this is Andrew, half of our five-star crew."

I offered Andrew my hand as the meaning of Van's introduction settled over me.

I am his fiancée.

Why then am I obsessing over the name Madison?

"Ms. McGrath, it's a pleasure." Andrew tilted his head toward the cockpit. "Let me introduce my wife, Ruth."

A petite woman seated in the pilot's seat turned, smiled, and waved. She too wore a uniform similar to Andrew's. "Good morning. It won't be long now."

"Andrew and Ruth make the perfect crew," Van explained. "They don't mind when my travels entail staying in different places. They both worked for commercial airlines before coming to Sherman and Madison, and now they can travel together. We're lucky to have them."

I tried not to let my thoughts linger on how easily the name Madison flowed from Van's lips. It's simply a name.

Ruth spoke, pulling my attention her way. "It's nice to meet you, Ms. McGrath." She grinned. "Maybe you could talk Mr. Sherman into someplace more exotic and warmer than Chicago."

The unease that I'd felt out on the tarmac faded

with the friendly conversation. "I'll work on that," I said. "Chicago wasn't my first choice either."

Van led me to two soft leather seats facing one another on one side of the plane. After laying our satchels on the seats to our side, we both sat down, our knees almost meeting in the middle. Van lowered his volume. "I don't know if you've noticed, but I'm a minimalist when it comes to employees, especially to those who have access to me and now to you. There's no regular flight attendant." He shrugged. "Unless we're flying a larger group, I'm perfectly capable of making my own cup of coffee or unwrapping a sandwich."

"I've noticed and I don't mind." A grin curled my lips. "I prefer the privacy." A thought about Skylar came to mind. I'd almost said that I liked the change, how everything with my ex felt like a grand performance always in need of an audience—a room full of people or employees. It was the visibility that mattered.

I didn't.

Skylar was my past.

Van didn't need to hear me talk about him any more than I already had.

Laying my head against the soft seat, I closed my eyes, trying to decide why my mind was in a funk. I could blame it on our early rising but not on the way Van woke me or the way our lovemaking continued under the warm water of our morning shower.

The extended session threatened to make us tardy

for our arrival at the airport and then for our morning meeting in Chicago. Van wasn't the one to blame.

It was me.

Holding his neck, my ankles locked behind his back and my breasts pressed against his solid chest, I was sandwiched between him and the tile.

It was as if I'd awakened this morning starved for affection.

I couldn't get enough—I needed to feel him, to know we were real. I needed the sensation of his skin against mine, the hunger of his kiss, and stretch of his cock within me. For longer than had become my normal, my orgasm stayed close and yet out of my reach.

The promise of relief seemed unobtainable as my fingers blanched his skin. Van continued to thrust, creating friction in the best of ways. My back arched and my fingers linked behind his neck as the warm water continued.

I didn't want our union to end, to lose that connection.

And then the orgasm hit, much like a freight train silently chugging through the darkness, not making its presence known until it barreled through me with unmeasured ferocity, leaving me ruined and spent. For moments I clung to his neck, my body still in his arms, and him still buried inside me. Soaked and exhausted, I wanted to climb back into my bed and relish the lingering aftereffects.

Thinking back, maybe Van was right. Perhaps I was worried about what awaited us in Chicago, in that world beyond our snow globe.

As the steps and door to the Cessna closed, Andrew appeared at our side. "The preflight checklist is complete. We're approved for takeoff as soon as another plane lands. We're still on schedule and should be wheels up in less than ten minutes. In the meantime, is there anything I can get either of you?"

"We're fine. Thank you for the timetable," Van said. He looked at his wristwatch. "That should mean we'll land before 8:30."

"Yes, sir. Ruth has confirmed that your car and driver will be waiting."

"Thank you."

By the time Andrew was back to the cockpit, Van squeezed my hand. "It's not a long flight, but you might consider taking off your coat and gloves."

His voice pulling me from a fog, I shook my head and began the task of removing my gloves and coat. "Of course," I muttered. Apparently, thoughts of our morning lovemaking had me a bit flustered.

Van took both of our coats toward the back of the plane where I watched as he hung them on hangers in a small closet.

"Our luggage is below," he said as he came back to our seats. "Would you like coffee? I remembered to have cream on board."

I shook my head and looked out the small window

as Van busied himself at a small workstation, one that moments earlier had been disguised as a cupboard. Soon he was again across from me. There was something in his grin and a twinkle in his green eyes that caught my attention as he stared my way.

"What?" I asked.

He leaned forward, tugging gently on a small curl dangling near my ear and smiled. "You're stunningly beautiful, Julia. I should tell you that a hundred times a day."

"You're thinking about the lace lingerie."

"I was thinking about our shower." His grin broadened. "However, now that you mentioned the lingerie, I'm thinking about taking it off you."

The rumble of his tenor sent shock waves to my earlier satisfied core and hardened my nipples. One thought led to the next. "I'm glad we have a hotel room."

His forehead furrowed. "What other option would we have?"

"When I told my parents we were coming to the city, Mom assumed we'd stay with them."

Van's laugh shattered the tension that had been growing within me.

"I doubt seriously that your parents want me to stay in their home."

"My mom would be all about showing it off."

"I'm not easily impressed." He placed his coffee in a cupholder and leaned forward, laying his hand on my knee. "I don't give a fuck about their house, Julia. It could be Buckingham Palace and I wouldn't care. I'm only impressed by one of your parents' accomplishments. And at this very moment, I'm staring into her beautiful blue eyes."

It would be easy to get lost in the way Van looked at me. Even on this plane and after what we'd done upon waking, his gaze was all-consuming. In his orbs it was as if in the entire world only I could satisfy his hunger and desire. "You make me feel..." I gripped the armrest as the plane began to move along the tarmac.

"I hope the rest of that sentence is something along the lines of *beautiful, wanted*" —he paused— "*loved*."

"I think it's more than that. Or less." I covered his hand on my knee. "You, Mr. Sherman, make me *feel*. That's the extent of the sentence and at the same time, it's overwhelming."

"Then by all means, a hotel suite is best because I plan to make you feel every chance I get."

I looked down at the way our hands had turned and the way our fingers had intertwined. Looking back up, I grinned. "Mom said you could have the guest room."

"Someday if we have a daughter, I hope for the young man's sake that I too am able to be as blind as your mother seems to be."

The sound of the engines revving with power created a dull roar.

"You want children?" I asked, realizing it wasn't a subject we'd ever discussed.

"You don't?"

"I guess I assumed..."

"Don't assume, Julia. I've told you that I've done things in my past that a better man would regret. You make me want to be more. Therefore, in answer to your question, yes, I'm open to children." His gaze simmered as the engine's hum grew louder and the plane lifted off the ground. "Especially if they see the world through their mother's eyes. I'm enthralled by your innocence and wonder."

"I think the ship has sailed on innocence." My cheeks warmed. "And you are the one responsible."

He shook his head. "Not like that. You see everything anew with wonder and delight. I imagine showing our children that life is filled with possibilities, and no one or nothing will hold them back." Letting go of my hand, he sat back. "Then again, it's fair to say a mini-me could test my patience."

The thought of a mini-Van made my smile grow.

Listening to Van speak about children, about *our* children, settled over me with all the comfort of a warm blanket. It wasn't because I was anxious to have children anytime soon. It was more about the fact that I wasn't ready to rule out the possibility. A conversation I'd had with Vicki came to mind. She'd asked about Van's age and if it bothered me.

His age didn't, and yet the possible limitations due to his age had been gnawing at me without me even realizing it. After all, if we were both younger, the world would be balanced.

Is that how it was with Madison?

Before I could give that more thought, Van pushed a button below the windows and a table appeared, filling the space between us. He reached for the leather satchel and removed his laptop. "This is what I wanted to show you before we land."

I took a deep breath.

Memories of lovemaking and discussions of limitless futures were done. It was time to do what I knew was my place and at the same time, somehow dreaded. It was time to get down to business. "About Wade?"

Van nodded. "You can do this, Julia. You were born to run Wade Pharmaceutical. Your interest in a more active role won't be met with unanimous enthusiasm. If I'm correct, Marlin Butler is prepared to ambush you."

Chapter 07

Julia

"Ambush me?" I repeated in question.

Van nodded. "Look at it from his point of view. Your sudden desire to take an active role in Wade Pharmaceutical is more than business to him. It's personal. You left his son at the altar. Because of you, his plans to profit from the company are ruined. You belong at the helm of Wade, and if Marlin is half the ass I know him to be, he'll use every opportunity to make that transition difficult."

"My grandfather's wishes can't be overturned by a shareholder."

"They can. I looked at your grandfather's will and discussed it with some of the best minds on my legal staff. The fulfillment of your grandfather's wishes is an assumption of norms."

My eyes narrowed. "Grandfather has been gone for nearly ten years. His will went through probate. It's set." I shook my head. "My dad wasn't happy that Grandfather changed the succession order of ownership of the family shares from him and Mom to me, but it's set.

And it was Grandfather who mandated that my mother take on the co-CEO position. All those things happened."

"Because your parents didn't fight them. Do you remember telling me that the stipulation in his will mandating that you marry is archaic and misogynistic?"

I had said that.

"And what did you say you could do?"

"Fight it...in court." Saying the words made them real. The information I'd read about Van, the hurdles he faced in court. My eyes opened wide. "Can Marlin fight the will in court? How? He doesn't stand to inherit. Those shares belong to me, to McGraths. It's what Grandfather wanted."

"Unfortunately, in the world of high finance, there are few absolutes."

"Help me understand."

Van took a deep breath and turned his computer screen toward me. "Any filings made in the courts are public record. When I spoke with your father the other day, I informed him of what my team had found."

"You didn't tell me."

"I'm telling you now. All that's visible—that is public at this point—is a petition to contest Herman Wade's last will and testament." He pointed at the screen. "I hadn't mentioned it before because I was hoping we'd have more information before heading to Chicago."

"Marlin is challenging my grandfather's will on what grounds?" I recalled learning about this subject in some class at Northwestern. It was a professor who liked to go down rabbit holes, ones that at the time seemed unimportant. I lifted my hand. "In the state of Illinois, the petitioner would need to challenge by questioning my grandfather's mental health. It wasn't in question."

Van nodded.

"Or he'd need to claim that the will is a forgery or fake or that a later will was written. The fact that my parents have followed the stipulations up until now should nullify that claim. And there's one more..." I tried to remember.

Van spoke, "There is also a challenge stating that an outside party exerted undue influence on the creation of the will and one stating that your grandfather was unaware of the contents of his will, which is not provable since he's passed."

I crossed my arms over my chest and leaned back. "Marlin can't prove any of those things."

Van's expression seemed unusually solemn. "The petition was filed by a large legal firm in Chicago, not the firm that Wade employs, and there isn't a name on the petition. It's the law firm Abbott and Jones versus the estate of Herman Wade."

I blinked as I tried to make sense. "When was this filed?"

"December 23rd. My team found it Monday, later than I would have liked. I wanted to know more before I told you."

"It has to be Marlin," I said.

"He makes the most sense. When I spoke to your father, he had no idea. The holidays are fucking with the flow of information. The courts closed the afternoon of the twenty-third. Those dealing with this particular litigation are on recess until January 3rd."

"Doesn't this sound like Marlin?" I asked. "He had the sale of shares planned for the holidays when Skylar and I would have been gone."

"It does, but I can't prove it." Van tilted his head. "He's almost too obvious."

My lips pursed before I replied, "Occam's razor." Sometimes the simplest explanation is the best one.

"There is that."

"My dad knows about the petition?"

Van nodded.

"And you still made the balloon payment yesterday?"

He nodded again.

"You said *versus the estate of Herman Wade*. That's all-encompassing." My skin prickled. "It's everything my parents have." Even I heard the desperation in my own voice. "Who would do this?"

Van leaned back against the chair as we floated above the clouds. "The fact that the filing came after our announced engagement means the list is rather exhaustive. As we've said, Marlin Butler is the first choice for obvious reasons, but Julia, he's not the only one. My team and I will get to the bottom of this."

"Who wants to hurt my parents?"

"They may not be the target."

"Me?" I questioned.

"Indirectly, me. I've made enemies."

"Doesn't the filer need to have a financial interest?"

Van nodded. "Have you read your grandfather's will?"

As I shook my head, the reality hit me. I hadn't.

"He named a long list of charitable contributions. It isn't unheard of for charities to question the value of an estate. Those benefactors cast the list of possible suspects wide open."

When I didn't reply, Van added, "Our engagement and the precariousness of Wade revealed vulnerability in my shield. I told you that I have a team who constantly searches for vulnerable companies. I'm not the only person who does that. Think of this as if it were nature. A healthy rabbit can still be a wolf's meal. An injured rabbit will be devoured."

"Wade was injured by the press and even more so when the lending institution demanded the balloon payment." I didn't ask. I knew it to be true.

"If that rabbit could retreat to its burrow and recover, it may stay safe." He blinked as his nostrils flared. "I exposed Wade. Unintentionally, I exposed its susceptible status."

"But it's not weak any longer. The perceived value has increased, and you paid the balloon payment early."

"The court filing was before most of that happened."

"Tell me what I'm walking into when we meet with the executive board."

Van took a deep breath. "An uneasy environment. There are a lot of unknowns—variables. You need to walk into this meeting confident in the knowledge you have. One, the balloon payment was made. Two, your impending nuptials will result in the fulfillment of your grandfather's stipulations."

"What about the petition against the will?"

"It may be brought up, but if it is, respond without urgency. While you're aware of it, the filing is irrelevant at this time. That process will take time. If there's one thing I've learned over the years about the courts, it's that they move at a snail's pace. The filing of the petition is only the first step. According to your father, your parents haven't been notified. Also, the fulfillment of the stipulations will solidify the legal document, making it more difficult to challenge."

"My—*our* marriage?"

Van nodded.

I let out a long breath. "Who else knows about the petition?"

"It depends on who your father's told."

"I want to talk to him first—privately."

"There isn't much time. The meeting with the board is set for ten a.m." He looked at my satchel. "Didn't you mention that you and your father have a secret way of communicating?"

I felt my grin surface as I nodded.

"Email him. Arrange a private meeting. Even if it's only for fifteen minutes. A unified front will show the willingness of the McGraths to stay the course and make it beyond this vulnerable time. Think about the Alzheimer's research."

"I didn't get the information I asked to receive."

"That's another reason we're going to Chicago. Marlin Butler held up the transfer of the files. He and I are going to talk."

"You won't be with me when I meet with my dad?"

Van reached for my hand. "Julia, I have faith in you. Remember the way you spoke to your parents and Skylar on Christmas day?" He didn't let me answer. "You are a force. I see it. You need to believe it. Let your father and the entire executive board see you the way I do. Let them sense your confidence. I'll tell you a secret I learned along the way."

"I'm listening."

"Most people are fucking scared." He leaned forward. "People collectively and individually. The way humans are wired creates a psychological need to latch onto someone who isn't frightened, someone who makes them feel the calm, not the storm. It's not a conscious thought. It's psychological and physiological. It's survival of the fittest. When you address your dad, be that calm. When you speak with the board and hear their concerns, reassure them with your words as well as your demeanor." A smile pulled at his full lips. "You, Miss McGrath, will blow them away."

"I think I should write that quote in your memoir."

"You'd have to credit Lennox. That man is self-assured and the definition of tranquil all rolled into one."

"Where do you think he learned it?"

"If I'm to believe the relatively clear evidence, his family has criminal associations that probably helped create a believable façade."

My eyes opened wide. "Oh, can I write about that?"

"No, beautiful. That would be redacted. I have enough enemies without adding a powerful crime family to the list."

"It would sell books."

Ruth came our way from the cockpit. "Excuse me. We're about to begin our descent. Please be sure to have your seat belts buckled."

"Thank you, Ruth," Van replied.

Chapter 08

Van

I covered Julia's hand with mine as the Chicago cityscape passed by the windows of the hired car. As Chicago is one of the larger cities in the country and not a great distance from Ashland, I come here often for business. There was a time that a small neighborhood on the outskirts of this city was my home. Living in the heart of a city never appealed to me.

My thoughts weren't on the past or even the scheduled meetings. My mind was consumed with Julia, a complete about-face from my thoughts that usually preceded an important meeting.

I wasn't unprepared. I'd adequately done my research for my meeting with Marlin. I'd purposely scheduled it for after the meeting with the executive board. I'd also done my homework on the board members. The thing about a privately owned company, the executive board and the shareholders tended to be one and the same. While like larger companies where the shareholders elected the board members, there are fewer candidates.

Wade Pharmaceutical has had the same board members since Herman Wade's passing: co-chairs Gregg and Anastasia McGrath; vice chairs, Marlin and his wife, Gwen Butler; and secretary, Elenore Rose. In essence, Julia was walking in on her parents and Skylar's parents three days before the date of her canceled wedding.

It was no wonder she had doubts.

The recent shuffle of Wade Pharmaceutical shares made one particular member of the board stand out, Mrs. Rose. I didn't know much about her other than she and her late husband were friends of Julia's grandparents. They willingly purchased fifteen percent of Wade shares when the company was first privately divided. Mr. Rose passed away five years ago after a long battle with Alzheimer's. Now at eighty-two years of age, Mrs. Rose was more than happy to sell her shares and move on. The transaction was all set for Marlin Butler's taking until I swooped in, offering her twenty-five cents more on the dollar.

Gregg McGrath told me that she offered her resignation from the board following this emergency meeting. It will then be up to the board to reach out to all shareholders, old and new, and ask for nominations. I personally know the owner of Aphrodite Corp. would jump at the chance to work Wade from the inside.

It's GreenSphere that had me at a loss. Despite two

days of digging, I had no information on the people behind the SPAC.

"Is there anything you can think to ask me?" I asked. "Anything that you think will be helpful with your father or the board."

Her blue stare came my way. "You're going to be with me for the board meeting."

She didn't ask, but I answered. "Yes, and I'll do what I did on Christmas, say as much or as little as you need."

"Is that how you succeed at what you do?"

"Yes. I've walked into meetings and eliminated entire departments, fired vice-presidents—most companies are top-heavy. And I've done it all without excessive explanation. When it comes to dollars and cents, no one gives a shit about flowery words."

She sighed. "I don't have questions for you, but I do for the board and for Dad. Marlin will have every reason to treat me as less if I'm without information." She sat taller. "Van, when are we headed back to Ashland?"

"If I had my say, I'd take you back this afternoon and keep you locked away" —I ran my finger over her cheek — "in a place that didn't make you stressed."

Or me.

Lena's concerns over Logan Butler and Phillip had me thinking. Ashland was one place, but in Chicago, we were vulnerable. Michael, the driver taking us to the Wade Pharmaceutical executive offices, was also a bodyguard, one from an established security firm that Connie found. Michael wasn't working alone for me. He was the most visible. There were three others who would have their eyes and ears on us whenever we were out of the hotel suite.

On top of that, my private detective was currently checking on my dear brother and confirming that he was in Texas with his daughter where he belonged.

"I know what I want to say to the board," Julia said.

"Go on."

"I want to tell them that I intend to follow my grandfather's stipulations. I'll confirm our engagement and explain that you paid the balloon payment and will pay the one due in sixty days if needed, but here's what I know I need to do..."

With each word, each sentence, and each phrase, Julia's confidence was building. I saw it in her straightening posture, heard it in her voice, and felt it in the air. Fuck, the way she took on life was addicting to watch and to experience.

"I'm going to demand the files regarding the new research. I want it all. I want everything from the R&D concept proposal through the up-to-the-minute research. I want to know how much Wade has spent and what the projections are for future expenditures." She reached for my arm. "More than that. We need profit-and-loss reports going back at least five years. Oh, and bank statements, records of our payments and debts."

I couldn't hide my smile at her growing enthusiasm.

"I want to know why the bank lost confidence. My gut says it's more than the cancellation of my wedding."

I nodded. "And you want to stay here in the city to go through everything?"

"I do." Her expression clouded. "If you need to get back to your office, I understand. I think I'd like to stay at the hotel."

I had no intention of leaving Julia in Chicago alone; nevertheless, I asked, "Why not stay at your parents'?"

"Because when I'm there, they see me as their child. I need the separation." She shrugged. "In all honesty, when I'm under my parents' roof, I see myself as their child too."

"I'm not leaving you." I pounded out a text message and hit send. "We'll stay in a suite. We can both work from there. Hell, I may even use this opportunity to do more in-person meetings that I wouldn't do in Ashland. Connie and my staff can hold down Sherman and Madison. I'll be as in touch as I would be from the house."

Julia blinked away the glassiness in her gaze. "You'll stay here with me? I don't know how long it will take to go through all of that information, and once I do, I want to meet again with the board."

I nodded.

"There's something else," she said.

"What?"

"Diving into Wade means I'll need to put your memoir on the back burner for the time being."

I again reached for her hand. "Didn't I tell you that you were the first applicant to actually show for an interview?"

"You did."

"I think the memoir can wait. My life story isn't going anywhere."

"It is, Mr. Sherman."

"It is?" I asked for clarification.

"Yes, you are now engaged to someone who because of you believes she can actually make a difference in her family's company, someone who feels as if she's started a brand-new life, all because of you."

I didn't deserve credit, but it was nice to hear. "How do you feel about facing the Butlers?"

Julia took a deep breath as her lips came together. "Better than I did this morning."

"I didn't tell you that I expected an ambush to frighten you. I did it to prepare you."

"And you did, Van. You have been honest with me even when you knew it might frighten me. I'm not only talking about Wade; however, for the moment, that's where I need to concentrate. The thing is that you've been honest with me from the beginning and never treated me as someone to be dismissed or too young to understand."

"You are young and beautiful and intelligent and a quick learner, and all of the pieces that when combined make my heart swell. If I were romantic, I'd say I'm seeing you as a delicate, rare flower." I fought the need to tease the cuff of her coat and blouse to confirm that the marks left behind from the belt were fading. Our gazes met. "In the last few weeks, your petals have opened, making you more confident and self-assured."

Julia grinned. "I'm not sure if that's romantic or philosophical. Either way, I'll take it."

I lifted her left hand. Even though it was covered by her gloves, I knew her ring finger was bare. "While we're in the city, I say we take time to buy you a ring."

"I'm not worried about a ring. I had one. I took it off."

"You won't take this one off."

"You seem rather confident, Mr. Sherman," she said with a smile.

"I am."

With Julia's hand still in mine, I gave it a squeeze as Michael pulled the sedan to the side of the busy street. We both looked up at the tall building that housed Wade Pharmaceutical's executive offices. The labs, manufacturing facilities, and distribution centers were scattered farther away in the suburbs.

"Is your dad ready to see you?" I asked.

"He knows I'm coming."

I kissed her forehead. "Later, at the hotel, there will be lots of coming."

A soft rose filled her cheeks, taking away her earlier look of worry.

Michael came around, opening the back door closest to the sidewalk. "Here you are, Mr. Sherman.

Wade Pharmaceutical corporate offices are on the forty-seventh floor." He tipped his chin toward the building. "Everyone is in place."

I nodded, knowing he was talking about his security team.

"Let's go," I whispered as I got out of the car and offered Julia my hand. Once we were both out and standing on the sidewalk, I spoke to Michael, "I'll call you when we're ready to leave. Connie will text you our hotel information."

"Yes, Mr. Sherman. She already has. We're prepared."

With my hand on Julia's back, we approached the glass entry.

I'd do as I'd promised, but if at any moment I believed Julia wanted or needed my input, it would be there. If it wasn't for her, I'd burn Wade Pharmaceutical to the ground just to watch the Butlers go up in flames. Fuck, I'd invite Lena and we would roast marshmallows.

That wasn't what would happen.

I'd make sure that Wade succeeded for Julia. That didn't mean that the Butlers would be spared from my revenge. A tingle reverberated through me. I hadn't spoken to Marlin Butler since his brother Logan had the audacity to overstep his bounds with Lena. I'd warned both Butlers that the time would come when I'd watch them fall.

The time had come.

Julia

*V*an gave my hand a squeeze before I stepped into my father's office, leaving Van in the front with Janie, my father's secretary. She'd been with him as long as I could remember. Long ago, before my mother also had an office in this suite of offices and my grandfather was still alive, I'd come into Dad's office and Janie would let me help her with filing and even typing.

Those memories and more came back as we greeted one another, and I introduced her to Donovan. It was Van's encouragement that helped me to no longer see myself as the little girl playing office but as an adult ready to take on the responsibilities that would help Wade succeed.

Dad smiled as he came around his desk, and I closed the door behind me.

He didn't say a word as he wrapped his arms around me.

In the short time it took him to reach me, I couldn't help but notice the way this recent ordeal had affected him, or maybe it was accumulative. There were more wrinkles and dark circles under his eyes. I took a step back and looked up at him. "Dad, are you okay?"

His appearance told me he wasn't.

Why hadn't I noticed the toll the stress had taken when I saw him a few days ago?

"I'm good, little girl."

He was holding my hands. "I'm here, Dad, because I'm done being the little girl. I care about the future of Wade, and I'm ready to be more involved. I don't plan on letting anyone else run my future."

Exhaling, Dad took a step back. "Is this you talking or is it Mr. Sherman?"

"It's me. The recent troubles made me realize how important this company is to me. And I was thinking about Mrs. Rose. Does she know about the research that's happening?"

Dad's smile faded as he nodded. "Technically, she's no longer a shareholder and has given notice of her resignation. She's ready to spend her last years enjoying life, not worrying about balloon payments and perceived value or possible litigation."

"Not a shareholder?"

"She sold to Mr. Sherman." He shrugged. "She didn't know that. He didn't reveal his identity, but we now know."

"Why wouldn't she come to you to sell?"

His eyes dimmed. "The important thing is that we now know the identity of most of the shareholders."

Most?

I took the seat in front of his desk. Instead of walking back to his chair, Dad sat at the seat beside me. I spoke first. "Van told me about the petition regarding Grandfather's will."

"He told me too." Dad let out a sigh. "We wouldn't have known were it not for his people."

"Who do you think it is?"

"Marlin believes it's him."

"He's confessing?" I asked.

"No, Julia. Marlin thinks Sherman filed the petition."

I sat straighter. "What? That doesn't make sense. He just paid the balloon payment." My volume rose. "Seven hundred and fifty thousand dollars. Why would he file a petition to challenge Grandfather's will? What would he stand to benefit?"

Dad looked at his watch. "The meeting of the executive board will begin in seven minutes. After the reading of the minutes, I'll introduce you and your...Mr. Sherman. You have as much time as you'd like to address the board."

"Pretty soon, I'll be part of that board."

"It's an elected position, but I don't see why you wouldn't. There are some new shareholders." He shook his head. "Everything is changing."

I reached out and laid my hand on his. "Change isn't necessarily bad. This change means that I'll take my rightful place."

"Not to push what I don't want pushed," he said, "but you can't take that place without a marriage license."

"I know, but I can prepare. And the marriage will happen."

Dad leaned against the soft upholstery chair back. "I'm tired, little girl. I've been working for a long time and your mother and I were talking. We don't know how long it will take until the new formula we're working on will become cleared for use or profitable. The assholes in Washington are trying to make changes to the way Medicare pays for different medications. Alzheimer's is predominantly a later-in-life disease. We need Medicare yet we still don't get the reimbursement we do from private insurance. We're barely getting by. We aren't. You know that."

"What are you saying?"

"I'm saying that maybe now, with the payment made and hope on the horizon, it's time to sell or maybe there's another answer."

I jumped from the chair. "No."

"We could get a better price if we leak the Alzheimer's rumors."

"You've always been against Big Pharma."

"I still am. I received a call yesterday that has me thinking."

"No, Dad."

"It was from a smaller pharmaceutical company out of Indianapolis, Sinclair Pharmaceuticals. They've been working on a game-changing compound to help with PTSD. Damien Sinclair called, owner to owner. He believes we could work out a merger. Both of our facilities are moderate in size. Together we could push for a larger share of the market."

I shook my head. "No."

"That's how the big companies, Pfizer, Roche, and Merck to name a few, became large. Two companies merged to become one. They added another and another. Maybe if we merge, we won't lose our autonomy."

My head was still shaking. "Don't do this. Van's payment bought us time. Let's use it."

"The decision will be up to the executive board."

"It's Marlin, isn't it? He's pushing to sell. He wanted to sell before. What Skylar said about a wedding gift is bullshit and you know it. Marlin wants out and especially now that Van is involved."

"I agree that Marlin isn't happy about Mr. Sherman."

"Fine," I said. "Then he and Gwen can sell their shares. You heard Van offer to buy them the other night at his house. We don't need the Butlers. Let's get Wade back to where the decisions aren't up to a board of different families but one family. One, Dad. Ours."

"And Mr. Sherman."

"Yes, when we marry, he'll be part of this family."

"Waiting could lower our value."

"Or it could raise it. I know I'm not a scientist, but I can read balance sheets, cash flow and equity statements. I can look at our spending from a new and fresh perspective. Van will help me."

Dad's head shook again. "Marlin is against it."

"Fuck Marlin."

My father's eyes opened wide. "Little girl."

"I need your help. Convince Mom and the Butlers to stick it out at least two more months until the next payment." I stepped closer. "Come on, Dad. You've given your soul to this company. We have new shareholders. I want to know them too. I want all the information, everything including the progress on the research and development and how much we're spending on that. I'll stay here in Chicago and devote my time to making this work."

"You'll stay here at home?"

"Here in Chicago. Van and I will be staying in a hotel."

Dad didn't respond.

"Give me a week or two to learn what I can and meet again with the board. Today I'll tell them my vision. I'll capitalize on Van's financial assistance, and I'll tell them what I need. It isn't up to Marlin Butler alone to sink this ship or to deny me the information that as a major stockholder is within my rights to request."

"You aren't a stockholder yet."

"Van is. He has one more percent than Marlin." When Dad didn't respond, I took a deep breath and lifting my hands, allowed them to slap the sides of my thighs. "Illinois has no waiting period before they issue a marriage license. If it will keep the board from agreeing to merge or sell..." I took a deep breath. "Van and I will marry today."

My father stood. "No."

"I don't need your permission."

"The challenge to your grandfather's will..." He turned away, walking to the bookcases along one wall and back. "If the plaintiff wins, if Herman's will is questioned, your mother and I...and you" —he added— "could lose everything."

"That won't happen."

"Don't you see? If we take Damien Sinclair's offer, we can't lose what we don't fully own."

"Dad, your logic is flawed. First, what's contestable about Grandfather's will?"

He stood straight. "I won't involve you in this, Julia. If it goes down, I'll take the responsibility."

My eyes narrowed. "What are you talking about?"

Before he could answer, there was a knock on the door.

"Come in," my dad called, jumping at the change in subject.

Janie looked at him and smiled at me. "Gregg, the meeting is about to start."

Dad reached for my hand. "Talk to the board. You have passion that we haven't had in a long time. I suppose you need to try."

"I do, Dad. I need to try."

He walked away, his shoulders slumping in a way I never before noticed.

Gathering my coat and bag, I followed him out to Janie's office as my eyes met the incredibly handsome green gaze coming from the man I loved, in the waiting area.

Van set his tablet down and came toward me. We met somewhere in between.

"Are you ready?" he asked, his deep tenor washing through me.

"I am and more determined than before."

Chapter 10

Julia

Silence settled over the boardroom as I completed my presentation. The information was out, Van had bought Wade time with the balloon payment. As the upcoming largest shareholder, I wanted information, all of it.

As of yet, I'd felt less as if I'd been ambushed and more as if I were being dismissed.

Marlin Butler glanced my way and back to the rest of the board. "If this is done, I move that we proceed with other items on our agenda."

"Second," Gwen said. She'd yet to meet my gaze.

"It isn't done," I said. "I want access to the information regarding my family's company."

"The motion was seconded," Marlin said.

I turned to Van, seated to the side of the room. There was something in his casual demeanor that calmed me. There wasn't a trace of anxiety anywhere from his tantalizing green stare to his handsome and fit body. Wearing a custom made suit that fit him perfectly, he looked as if he were watching a tennis match, leaned back with one arm outstretched over the back of a neighboring chair.

It hit me.

Van's demeanor was the manifestation of the secret he'd told me. People instinctively gravitated toward calm. There was no doubt I wanted to go to him, wrap myself around him, and settle into his orbit.

I grinned as our gazes met.

Van didn't want me to come to him, not now. He was showing me what I needed to do. I took a deep breath. My realization had taken only seconds as Marlin spoke.

"Thank you, Miss McGrath."

"Thank you for listening," I said with all the tranquility I could muster. "As I mentioned, I'm not done. Take a vote." When no one spoke, I added, "I motion that a vote be taken on my proposal to release the requested information to me."

"You are not in a position—"

My father stood. "As co-chair, I call for a vote."

I let out a breath, concentrating on Van's encouraging words. 'When you speak with the board and hear their concerns, reassure them with your words as well as your demeanor.'

I lifted my hand. "Before the vote, I would like to hear concerns. I'd like to understand any obstacles that any one of you may see with my having the information I've requested."

Gwen cleared her throat.

I feigned a smile. "Please, Gwen, share."

"I can't believe I'm being made to say this," she began, "but it's the obvious elephant in the room, Julia. You can't be trusted to use good judgment. You flew off the handle over a misunderstanding with Skylar. You committed to being his wife and changed your mind. Thousands of dollars wasted. Who is to say that you won't do the same with Wade. Just change your mind. Last I was told, you were setting Wade aside to write a memoir. Now I assume you're setting the memoir aside to concentrate on Wade. Or are you managing both? I really don't know. I do know that your track record doesn't instill confidence."

I licked my lips and took a deep breath. "Thank you for your honesty. This isn't, however, the time or the place to rehash what occurred regarding my broken engagement. This is the time to concentrate on Wade. The memoir isn't a topic for this board either. Wade is. I was raised to fulfill my grandfather's wishes, to be an involved and integral part of the company his father founded. If you truly have the best interest of Wade at heart, you'll see that Donovan Sherman saved your asses. He's presented on a silver platter an opportunity to save this company, to make it more. He also exposed the vulnerability of our shares. We are now down to fewer shareholders. Once Donovan and I combine our shares, we'll hold a number that surpasses the majority." I relaxed my shoulders. "This is my legacy, and I'm not willing to let it go without a fight."

"Perhaps," Gwen said, "if you'd shown better judgment in the past."

"She's twenty-four years old," my father interjected. "She hardly has an extensive track record." He smiled my direction. "Julia has made some decisions that on the surface seemed rash; however, upon learning the circumstances, I admire her fortitude." He shook his head and turned toward Donovan. "I don't know Mr. Sherman."

Van nodded.

Dad went on, "But Julia is right. Making the balloon payment has given us a reprieve we wouldn't have otherwise had." He nodded. "I'm grateful to Mr. Sherman. Whether he and Julia marry isn't the issue, nor should it be pushed. What matters is that Mr. Sherman has shown this board that he's sincere about helping Wade Pharmaceutical."

"For what purpose?" Gwen asked.

"I don't care," Dad answered. "I'm tired." He reached over to Mom and squeezed her hand. "I'm not a quitter and neither is our daughter. I vote to give her the information."

"How do we know," Marlin asked, "that she won't share it with the competition?"

"I won't," I said.

"Did you know that Donovan Sherman's portfolio includes Big Pharma stockholdings?"

My eyes widened as I turned toward Van.

Clearing his throat, Van stood, adjusting his suit

coat and smiling his ten-thousand-watt grin. "My portfolio is diverse, as is yours, Mr. Butler. Shall we discuss the extent of our investments? Perhaps this should be more inclusive, say, also the holdings owned by your wife, son, and brother?" Van pulled his phone from his pocket. "Only moments ago, I received a comprehensive list of those ventures." Van's head tilted. "Would you like me to share?"

Marlin stood, his hands on the table. "My investments aren't in question. I'm a trusted member of this board and have been—"

I lifted my hand, silencing Marlin. In all honesty, his muting himself was probably more out of surprise at my action than respect for me. "I still have the floor," I said. "Vote."

Dad lifted his hand. "In favor."

Next were Marlin and Gwen. They both voted against.

Mrs. Rose shook her head. "I'm sorry that I'm ineligible to vote."

Her words caught me off guard. Dad said she'd sold her shares and was resigning. I hadn't carried the thought to the next obvious conclusion. She couldn't vote.

"Julia, this is my last meeting," Mrs. Rose said. "I want you to know that I believe Herman and Juliette are smiling right now. What has always made Wade special was the family's passion. Listening to you today, I believe I'm leaving this seat and this board in good hands. You shouldn't only be on this board, young lady, but in power—the power your shares allot you."

"Thank you," I mouthed.

We all turned to my mother, who had been unusually quiet throughout my presentation. "Julia, I'm also pleased. I never thought you'd take this company seriously. I was wrong. Unfortunately, my vote in favor of providing you with the information you requested is useless. A vote must pass with a majority." She shook her head as my stomach dropped.

Fifty percent isn't a majority. Why hadn't I thought of that either?

"My vote is irrelevant," Mom said.

Van stepped forward and put his fingers on a notebook sitting on the table next to Mrs. Rose. "May I?" he asked before taking it.

Mrs. Rose practically blushed as Van graced her with a panty-melting smile. "Well, yes." She pushed it toward him.

Van flipped to the back of the notebook and tore a page from the binder. Next, he tore the page into four pieces and began to pass them out.

"Mr. Sherman, this is fruitless," Gwen said.

Van didn't stop until everyone had a quarter of the page. "Do you all have pens?"

"Yes." Came in murmurs.

Van turned to Marlin. "Regardless of how this turns out, you and I will be meeting alone."

Marlin's neck straightened.

Lifting his hands in a welcoming gesture, Van said, "Please vote. *Yes* indicates that you support supplying Ms. McGrath with the information she's requested. *No* indicates that you would deny Ms. McGrath information that is rightfully hers."

I shook my head as Van's gaze met mine. This wouldn't matter. I didn't understand why he was prolonging this ordeal. I wouldn't receive a majority. I had to find another way.

One by one, each person turned their paper over.

Slaps against the table reverberated through the room.

Van gathered the papers, shuffled them and handed them to Mrs. Rose. "If you'll be so kind," he said.

A bit flustered, Mrs. Rose reached for the papers and turned them over one by one.

"No." Her eyes met mine. "Yes." A slight grin came to her lips. "Yes."

"The next one is no," I whispered.

Mrs. Rose turned the paper. "Yes."

"What?" I asked, as a bud of hope sprang to life in my chest. "Really?"

"Marlin," Gwen said his name with all the shock and dismay she could possibly provide.

"It won't matter. Give her the information," Marlin said. "Our next vote is about the Sinclair offer. None of this will matter."

"Oh," Van said, "About that. I would suggest that you all check your emails. I believe Damien Sinclair has rescinded his original offer. You see, he decided that it would make more sense to ensure that Wade is profitable or at least has the potential before linking Wade and Sinclair Pharmaceuticals."

With each of Van's statements, my heart beat faster until it felt as if it would explode with gratitude. "How did you know about that?" I asked.

He winked my direction, wordlessly telling me what he'd said on the plane. Van would let me handle this until the time came that I needed him.

"If that is all," he said, "Ms. McGrath and I will wait for the conclusion to your meeting after which time, Mr. Butler, you and I will meet." He turned to my parents. "And Julia will meet with the two of you and receive the information she has requested."

Dad looked up from his phone and shook his head. "You interfered with the Sinclair offer."

"Mr. McGrath, I may not be a voting member of this board, but I do own a significant percentage of the shares. Yes, I communicated with Mr. Sinclair."

Dad looked across to the Butlers. "It seems as though our agenda has shrunk." He turned to Van and me. "We'll be done in a few more minutes."

With Van behind me, we exited the meeting room, closing the door behind us. The muffled sounds of discontent grew fainter as we stepped farther away.

"How did you do that?" I asked. "How did you know about Sinclair?"

"Janie is a lovely lady and quite talkative."

I shook my head in disbelief. "You just found out a few minutes ago and put a stop to the merger that fast? How and why?"

"It seems that not only does my portfolio contain investments in Big Pharma, but now it includes a recent investment in a small pharmaceutical company in Indianapolis." He shrugged. "Their PTSD research is interesting."

Chapter 11

Van

Nearly twenty years ago

Red. Scarlet. Crimson. Fiery.
Associated with heat.

The color of blood.

The color of rage.

The ruby hue colored my vision as I rode the elevator into the sky, the damn thing moving too slowly. My teeth clenched and my jaw tightened as I watched the numbers above the door change, one by one. At my sides, my fingers balled into fists and biceps bulged, itching to make contact, to feel destruction as my knuckles pounded into anything, even the walls surrounding me.

A quick glance at my phone told me it had been forty minutes since her call. It was the middle of the night. Hearing the fear in her voice took my breath away. I'd sprung from my bed, hurriedly dressed, and took off to the garage.

If only I'd been closer.

The elevator finally came to a halt.

With each millisecond, I contemplated prying the damn doors open with my bare hands. As soon as the space between them widened enough for my passage, I pushed my way through. At this time of night, more accurately, morning, the hallways of the large tower were blissfully empty. My pace quickened and my strides grew longer as I raced toward her door.

"Fuck, Lena. Tell me you didn't let him in." It was the chorus I'd said over and over as I made my way into the city and through Chicago's streets. Logan Butler. Even his name had me seeing red.

I gripped the doorknob.

The fucker didn't budge.

Digging deep in the pocket of my pants, I found the ring, the one with a single key. I pushed it toward the keyhole, forcing it in the lock. I could have broken the damn thing, but it didn't work. The lock was changed. "Fuck him."

My fists found satisfaction as I banged on the door, yelling her name.

"Lena, let me in."

My pulse raced as noises came from within the apartment. I waited as the locking mechanism clicked and the doorknob moved. As the door moved inward, I took a step forward only to be stopped by the one man I didn't want to see. Dressed in only boxer shorts, he was older and weaker than me. "Let me in, you sick fuck."

"Go away, Thomas." Logan Butler smirked.

"Get the fuck out of my way."

"You're not coming in."

"Like hell I'm not." My chest grew as I squared off. "Who's going to stop me. Not you."

Lena's voice came from the dark apartment behind Butler. "Van, go."

Using my foot and arm, I pushed the door from Logan's grasp and stomped past him into the shadows. "Lena, where are you?"

Minus the light coming through the windows with the night sky and the city below, the apartment was dark, obscuring every corner.

I called out her name again as Logan's hand landed on my shoulder.

He spoke, his words were there, hanging in the tense air, saying something about paying for his time. I didn't listen nor did I give a fuck as I swung, my fist contacting Logan's cheek. His head snapped back and to the side. Pain shot through my fist, my nerve endings exploding.

It was exactly what I needed.

An outlet.

I didn't stop, swinging again. The relief in each impact egged me on, fueling my need for destruction. Logan tried to fight back—I'd give him that—but he was no match for me. With him pinned against the wall, I continued my assault, following him toward the floor as his legs gave out.

The red coloring my vision now ran down Logan's face and over my hands.

Punch after punch.

"Van, stop," Lena said as she reached for my arm.

Her pull was nearly nonexistent. Nothing more than a butterfly landing on a flower. It was the tone in her voice that affected me, that caused me to stop, to turn, and to see the woman before me. In the cunning world of lies, deceptions, and money, Lena and I found one another. Our common goals of power and unimaginable wealth should have made us enemies. Instead, somehow, they'd united us.

Lena and I didn't have a relationship made of romance or love, not in the true meaning of the words. Sex wasn't our connection. Our bond went to our core —our common love of someone else.

I spun around, cupping Lena's face, momentarily ignoring Butler's blood on my hands but seeing Lena's blood, dried and caked upon her alabaster skin, the purple of the bruise on her left cheek. Leaving red fingerprints on her cheeks, I took a step back, reached for her hands, and lifted her arms. Her painted fingernails were jagged.

She'd given him hell.

The purple fingerprints on her wrists and arms confirmed she'd gotten it too.

"I'm fucking suing you, Thomas," Butler said, lying against the wall, spitting more blood down his bare chest and on Lena's marble floor.

"He did this," I said to Lena, not questioning but wanting to hear it from my friend.

"I..." she looked down. "Infidelity."

"Fuck that company." I turned to Logan Butler. "The contract isn't in your name. You have no rights to her."

Butler groaned as he stood. "This is my apartment. My name's on the damn lease. I bought out the contract from Nicholson." His beady stare lingered too long on Lena. "She's mine for another six months."

I stepped in front of her. "Tell that to the cops when they arrest you on domestic violence charges."

"You're the one going down."

"Fucking try," I said, reaching for Lena's arm, rougher than I should. "Go get your things." Taking a breath, I loosened my grip. "You're coming home with me."

Lena's brown eyes searched from me to Logan and back.

"Go," I repeated.

"If you walk out of here, Lena," Logan said, "you're not coming back. I'll call Infidelity. I'll get back every fucking dime I paid. You'll owe me hundreds of thousands."

"You didn't pay," I reminded him, "not directly to Infidelity. You have no say on what happens. And what you just did nullifies the contract. I take Lena to the hospital, and she presses charges, Infidelity won't refund your money. You'll lose either way."

A slimy smirk quirked his lips as he used his hairy arm to wipe away the blood still coming from his nose. He spoke to Lena, but he was looking at me. "Maybe I'll fuck with your sister instead."

My neck straightened and my clenched jaw threatened to splinter my teeth with the pressure. It wasn't *my* sister, Olivia, that he was talking about but Lena's. Her younger sister. The real reason Lena had entered into a contract with the companionship service, Infidelity. She'd been promised that Infidelity didn't sell sex; it sold class, poise, companionship, and compatibility.

I took a step closer. "Get the fuck out of here before I pound you to a bloody pulp. When I'm done, even your brother won't recognize you."

"Touch me again, Thomas, and jail is the only place you're going."

I smirked. "Maybe they'll let us share a cell. Just so you know, I'll top."

I turned to Lena.

It was the first time I'd noticed that she was wearing a long satin nightgown with a matching robe that hung from her slender shoulders. Her feet were bare, her painted toenails peeking out from the hem of the nightgown. "Put on clothes. Grab what you want. You're coming with me. I'm not leaving without you."

My expression and tone left no room for argument.

Finally, Lena nodded and turned away toward the bedroom.

When Logan began to protest, screaming demands

her direction, I pushed the fucker against the wall with my forearm at his neck. The pressure to his windpipe caused his beady eyes to bulge. "You like to beat up girls, fucker? If she or Madison so much as has a scratch because of you, I'm coming after you. I'm taking you down. I'm going to watch as you lose everything."

I let up as Logan gasped for breath. "You've had some success." He shook his head. "You're still nothing. You're Donovan Thomas, a wannabe. In what world do you think you can beat me? Having an office and wearing a suit doesn't make you anything more than a cheap used-car salesman. If you leave with Lena, I'm nullifying the contract."

Good.

"You won't," I said, "because it's what she wants, and you're too much of a conniving asshole to do anything for anyone else. I don't give a fuck about the contract. As we've established, it's with Nicholson, not you. From all my research, I've determined that Infidelity isn't about sharing. They have their reputation to worry about too. Nicholson broke his part of the contract by subletting his agreement."

Fuck, it sounded like Lena Montgomery was an apartment or a possession such as a car or a boat. She wasn't. She was a person who wanted to survive the loss that Logan Butler was responsible for. She'd gone to him for help, professionally.

It became a relationship, one not defined by contracts. He'd offered to help her invest an insurance settlement. He did, but in the process, he stole what Lena and Madison had left of their parents.

She'd left his ass and gone to Infidelity, the one place she could possibly make back the money she'd lost. It was a ruse. Logan used Nicholson, helping him with the questionnaire, making him the perfect match for Lena. After the contracts were signed, Nicholson disappeared, handing Lena over to Logan.

"I'm ready," Lena said, now dressed in blue jeans and a top with a jacket. Her hair was pulled back and covered by a Cubs baseball hat. Despite the darkness outside, she wore sunglasses. In her arms, she hugged an overfilled leather backpack. "Here." She handed me a wet washcloth.

After wiping Logan's blood from my hands, I tossed the cloth at him and pointed my finger. "Stay the fuck away from both of the Montgomerys."

"Aw, but they owe me." His teeth in his disgusting smile were red. "Madison is as sweet as sugar."

I stepped closer; my cadence slowed. "Listen closely, you motherfucker. Things have changed. Madison's my wife. If you get near her, I'll kill you."

Reaching for Lena, I placed my hand in the small of her back. As I did, I felt the object she had hidden. Her face snapped my direction, her closed lips begging me not to say a word. I didn't as we exited the apartment.

"You felt it?" she said softly as we waited for the elevator.

I nodded. I'd felt the butt of the pistol tucked into the back of her jeans.

"I was going to use it," she said, her voice growing stronger. "I had a plan. I was waiting until he fell asleep." Tears streamed from behind the sunglasses. "I would have killed him."

A rush of pride and admiration washed over me as we stepped into the elevator. "I believe you."

"I'm not a victim, Van. He was about to be."

I ran my palm over my face. The rush was over, leaving me exhausted. I exhaled. "You're kick-ass. I'll give you that. Why don't you use those kick-ass powers to bring him down in a way that won't end up with you behind bars?"

"Do you ever see it?" she asked.

"What?"

"The green. It was something I never realized existed when my parents were alive, but since Logan stole our money—our everything—I see the green everywhere."

The elevator stopped in the parking garage as I led Lena toward my car. "I'm not sure what you mean."

She reached for my hand, bringing us to a stop. "Look around."

Indulging her, I did, seeing rows and rows of cars.

"It's here," she said. "It's everywhere. It's the deep and aching sense that I want what everyone else has. What people like Logan and his family have. What people who can afford an apartment in this building and still drive cars worth more money than I've ever had."

I hadn't thought about it in those terms. Logan Butler's assessment of me came back—you're nothing. His words fueled my need to succeed.

When we were both in my car, I said, "Green envy."

Lena nodded.

"I'd never given it a color, but I get it. I see it more as an insatiable hunger. I can't be satisfied until I have more...everything."

She smiled, still wearing the silly sunglasses as I pulled out onto Lake Shore Drive. "One day."

"Fucking yes. We'll both make it."

"I know we will. More..."

"Everything."

Chapter 12

Van
Present day

Julia's and my conversation silenced as the sound of footsteps echoed from the hallway. We waited as someone entered, unobservant of his surroundings as he headed with purpose toward the closed door to the ongoing board meeting.

I reached for Julia's hand as she made a soft gasp.

It wasn't loud enough for Skylar to turn our direction, his intent set upon opening the door. Janie from Gregg's office stood from where she sat near the door. "I'm sorry, Mr. Butler, the meeting is already in progress."

"Janie" —he lifted a manila folder— "I have some information my father needs to see."

"I'm sorry. It will need to wait."

"This is pertinent information about Sinclair Pharmaceuticals." His shoulders relaxed. "Janie, would you take it in there? I promise the board needs this information."

She nodded. "Very well." Taking the folder from

Skylar, she knocked softly on the door, opening it, and speaking softly into the room.

It was then that Skylar turned, his eyes widening as his gaze was met by two people he evidently didn't anticipate. It would be accurate to say that I found humor in his evolution of demeanors.

Shock.

Anger.

Indifference.

Standing, I lifted my chin. "Mr. Butler. It seems you're on the outside looking in."

Ignoring me, his gaze was fixed on Julia. "I didn't believe that you'd really come, not back to Chicago, not days before our wedding."

Feeling her presence beside me, I didn't need to turn to know that Julia had also stood.

Her voice was as strong and sure as it had been in the meeting. "I suppose I could say the same thing."

"I live here, remember. I also work in these offices."

"For now," I said.

Skylar's gaze moved as if he'd just noticed me, the wheels turning as he put the pieces into place. "You." He was definitely looking at me. "You are the reason Sinclair rescinded the merger offer."

"If that was the important information you needed to give Marlin," Julia said, "he already knows. Van informed them all, telling them to check their emails."

Skylar shook his head. "You want to ruin Wade, don't you?"

"No," Julia replied. "I want to save Wade and keep it from being swallowed up by Sinclair or any other company."

Skylar squared his shoulders. "I don't care if you two marry. I really don't give a fuck, but I won't stand by and let you on the board of directors, either of you."

Julia's words were laced with amusement. "Were you magically granted some sort of power, Skylar? You have no control or say-so in who's on the board. You aren't a shareholder, your father is. It's sad to think I used to at least like you."

The door opened and Janie returned. "Mr. Butler, your father said thank you for the information."

Skylar's gaze narrowed. "He already knew it. I know." He turned to us. "Goodbye, I hope not to see you again, and for the record, I don't wish you well."

It was difficult not to laugh.

As soon as he disappeared behind the wall and down the hallway from which he'd come, I reached for Julia's hand. "As CEO, I think your first job should be cleaning house."

"Mr. Sherman," Janie said. "Mr. Butler, *Marlin Butler*" —she clarified— asked me to show you to his office. He'll be along in a moment."

Nodding, I gave Julia's hand one more squeeze. "I'll see you after you meet with your parents."

Janie smiled. "I was given a list of what you've requested, Julia. I'll be happy to help you once I return."

"My parents?"

"They'll be along shortly."

Julia nodded.

Janie led me through a few doors and hallways until we came to double smoked-glass doors. The nameplate on the side said Marlin Butler, Vice President of Operations.

Titles were overused. Vice-presidents multiplied in most companies like mice—litter after litter—making companies top-heavy. Ironically, most vice-presidents were as equally useful as mice, scurrying about and shitting all over the place.

After the greetings between Janie and Marlin's secretary, I was led to a set of solid double doors.

"Mr. Sherman, may I get you anything while you wait? Coffee? Water?"

"No, thank you."

Having me wait in Marlin's office was no doubt a power play, an attempt to impress me with some self-perceived sense of superiority. Glancing at the view of Chicago through his floor-to-ceiling windows, my mind went to something else. A grin and a shake of my head were the telltale signs of a pang of sympathy for Gwen Butler. With the size of his desk and square footage of windows, Marlin was obviously compensating for an inadequacy. Maybe a life of unfulfilled sex added to her earlier negative attitude.

Thankfully for Julia, when I found her on the side of the road, I not only saved her life, I also rescued her from a lifetime of sex with a Butler. From what little

Lena had shared about Skylar's uncle and Marlin's brother, Logan was nothing to write home about either.

If Marlin Butler wanted me envious of his position, he had a fucking far way to climb up the corporate ladder. No, when it came to the Butlers—Marlin, Logan, and even Skylar—the green-eyed monster had changed companions. I was no longer a twenty-something determined to make a difference.

I'd long ago left the Butlers in my dust.

Envy was their constant companion, not mine.

I didn't give a fuck how Logan saw me nearly two decades ago. Times had changed and so had I. I had more money, more power, and now Skylar's fiancée as well as their key to Wade Pharmaceutical.

I had no doubt that Skylar told his father that I'd offered double their worth for their stock in Wade. That was why Marlin wanted to meet in person. He was wise enough to avoid a paper or electronic trail of this conversation.

What Marlin didn't realize was that I was now the master playmaker. This meeting was merely agreed upon to drop crumbs leading him and his family to exactly where I wanted them. One day I'd have Butler's shares of Wade, but when that day arrived, I sure as hell wouldn't be paying him a substantial sum.

The door behind me opened.

"Have a seat, Mr. Sherman," Marlin said as he entered, closed the door, and gestured toward the chairs opposite his grandiose desk.

I took the seat, leaning back and unbuttoning my suit coat.

Marlin settled behind the desk, busying himself with straightening the blotter. Finally, he broke the silence. "I wasn't sure you'd make the trip."

"You asked and I was curious."

Marlin's back straightened as he sat forward. "You cost me millions, Sherman."

My lips quirked into a grin. "If that's why you asked me here, it really wasn't necessary. I'm well aware of the consequences that my acquisition of the Wade shares created. You were right. I didn't need to travel three hundred miles to personally witness your defeat."

"Always so arrogant even when you didn't have a pot to pee in."

I smirked. "By the way, Damien Sinclair informed me that you also invested in Sinclair Pharmaceuticals."

Marlin shook his head. "It was just for show. A leap of faith, showing Sinclair that I trusted him. I didn't do it for any other reason."

"You didn't believe that the merger would increase Sinclair Pharmaceuticals' value and you'd benefit from both sides?"

"The merger was a good opportunity. Wade was also approached by Zax Drugs." His head shook. "They're currently in the middle of litigation regarding opioids. It's not where Wade needs to be."

"It seems on that we can agree."

"The offer from Sinclair was sound. Another one probably won't come around."

"Wade will survive on its own," I said.

"Quid pro quo," Marlin said, leaning forward. "I made a gesture in good faith. I expect you to do the same."

He thinks I owe him?

"And what was that gesture again?" I asked.

"I helped Julia with my vote. It's your turn to reciprocate."

And there we had it, Marlin's real motivation behind his vote. "And what did you have in mind?"

"You heard Gregg. We're all getting tired. This company was supposed to unite our families. That's done. Make me an offer."

I leaned forward. "To be clear, you're asking me to make you an offer for your shares in Wade? You're willing to sell."

"Skylar mentioned..."

I nodded.

Marlin stood. "Understand, I'll only consider this for the right price."

Exhaling, I resumed my relaxed position against the chair. It was my ringside seat to Marlin's tightrope act, wanting to sell while at the same time not wanting to admit it.

"An agreement would fulfill your promise," he said, "the one to Gregg about Wade once again being a family-owned company."

"I'll have my legal team draw up a proposal."

"I need a number, Sherman, an offer."

"And as soon as I walk out of the room, you're going to call GreenSphere Opportunities, Aphrodite Corp., or Wolfe Acquisitions, or all three, and tell them I made an offer. Then you're going to sit back as counter-offers come your way."

Back to sitting in his chair, Marlin's smile grew. "You've done your homework."

"I tell you what," I said, "have your lawyer write me a proposal."

"My lawyer."

"You don't want to use Wade's legal team for obvious reasons. Logan still has his law license, I presume."

The color drained from Marlin Butler's face. "This is between me and you. Logan wants nothing to do with you as I'm sure you feel the same."

I didn't feel the same.

Julia unwittingly returned me to an unfinished fight that had stalled. I was nearly twenty years late. The players were the same. The rules had changed, or more accurately, the rule maker. I'd changed. This time I didn't plan on walking away until the Butlers were ruined.

Standing, I pulled a business card from my pocket and handed it Marlin's direction. "May I suggest that you proceed with your plan in reverse? Find out the bids you can get from the other investors and then call my office with a proposal. I'll make you an offer, for Julia."

Not taking the card, Marlin leaned back, sighed, and shook his head. "Pretty young thing, Julia McGrath. She's nothing but trouble. Skylar saw it. I'm not sure how or why you latched onto her, Sherman, but beware."

Tossing my card onto his desk, I refrained from laughing. "Beware of Julia?"

He stood and feigned a shiver. "Nothing against her looks. She makes pretty arm candy, but McGrath women tend to run cold...frigid...if you know what I'm saying. Skylar knew that. He just acted too quickly. He'll learn."

My thoughts were back to the earlier part of his comment.

McGrath *women.*

Plural?

Julia.

Anastasia, her mother?

If my assumption was correct, and Marlin had personal experience with a McGrath woman, then that meant there were additional McGrath secrets to reveal.

"Maybe," I said, "the trouble isn't the women. Maybe it's the inept men in their beds."

A red hue climbed Marlin's neck, bringing crimson to his already-ruddy complexion. He stood taller. "You don't belong here. You've climbed out of the gutters and dressed yourself up, but it doesn't change who you really are, Sherman."

I expected him to use the name Thomas. To his credit, he didn't.

"You don't belong with Julia."

A smile curled my lips. "And yet you're offering to sell me your shares of Wade." I turned to walk toward the door and turned back. "Do tell Logan I said hello. We must catch up."

As soon as I stepped out of the office and closed the door, I sent a text.

Expect a call. The bait is set.

I hit send.

A smiling emoji with bright red lips was the reply.

Chapter 13

Julia

"How did your meeting with Marlin go?" I asked as Van and I settled in the back seat of the sedan.

"As I expected."

"Is that good or bad?"

Van squeezed my hand. "It's unimportant. You were fantastic up there in front of the board, stating your case and making your demands."

Warmth bubbled within me at his words and also because of the access I'd been granted. It would take time to go through the information. Having the opportunity was what was important.

Sighing, I leaned my head against Van's shoulder. "I was ready to give up."

"Never give up, beautiful. You were calm and concise. When Gwen Butler began her—"

"Ambush," I interrupted, sitting up. "She was the ambush, not Marlin."

"I was going to say when she began her concerns, I watched you. You didn't let her rattle you. That's what she wanted. She wanted to upset you and get you agitated. Your calm was the opposite. I'm so proud of you." He leaned in close, leaving a chaste kiss on my forehead. "And so was your dad. I watched him watching you."

"I'm not sure what my mom thinks."

Van nodded. "She's more difficult to read."

"I thought the whole thing was for nothing when Mom said what she did. When Dad told me that Mrs. Rose had sold her shares and was resigning, it didn't occur to me that it would take the board to an even number and be impossible for me to receive the majority vote. If I had, I probably wouldn't have even tried."

"Then I'm glad you didn't consider it."

I turned toward him. "How did you know that Marlin would change his vote with a written ballot?"

"I didn't. I also wasn't certain what your mother would vote when given the opportunity to cast her ballot anonymously."

"So why do it?"

Small lines formed around Van's eyes as his smile grew. "Because successful people don't leave opportunities untaken. And you, my love, are on the verge of immense success. You're that flower, opening her petals and showing the world how truly fantastic you are."

"I want to believe that."

"I wouldn't lie to you."

I shrugged, suddenly interested in a string on my

coat. "I feel different. Empowered. It's new, and I like it."

Van's gloved hand came to my cheek, turning me toward him. "It shows."

Our lips came together. Though the kiss wasn't passionate, the firmness of his lips against mine was the conduit sending his energy to me and mine to him. If we weren't in the back seat of a rented car with a driver we didn't really know, I would want more.

When we pulled away from one another, I grinned. "Thank you."

"The ballot was a long shot, but what would you have gained without it? If the answer was the same all that was lost was a few minutes. As it turned out, the answer changed. Opportunities are what we make."

I shook my head. "I know I said the memoir can wait, but I need to write some of what you say down."

My attention went out the windows of the sedan, seeing the city where I'd lived my entire life. I recognized the area and stores: Ann Taylor, Cartier, Burberry. There was an energy in this city that was invigorating and familiar. Even in late December, the streets were clogged with traffic and the sidewalks were filled with people.

When I turned back, Van was sending a message on his phone. When he stopped, I asked, "Where are we staying?"

"Somewhere where I can have you all to myself."

My smile grew as his words twisted my insides. "That doesn't narrow it down."

"Not at your parents' place."

"Still not narrowed."

I watched as Michael turned left on Delaware Place and then right on Rush Street. "The Waldorf?" I asked.

"The Terrace suite was available for an extended stay."

"Van, that's too much. I shouldn't have asked to lengthen our stay." I had an idea. "Let me pay for it."

Van's laugh echoed in the closed car. "I know you have money, Julia. So do I. Let me enjoy pampering you."

I peered out at the limestone structure. The historic hotel was considered one of the jewels of Chicago's Gold Coast.

"Our original reservations were at the Conrad. The suite was nice, but only had limited availability. It was after you asked about extending our stay that Connie found this possibility. If we're to spend a week or more in a hotel, we need space."

Inhaling, I peered out the windshield as Michael pulled into the circular driveway. Before our driver could get out, the bellman opened the door to my side.

"Welcome to the Waldorf Astoria, ma'am," he said, offering me his hand.

Van and Michael exchanged words I couldn't hear.

The winter chill disappeared as Van led me into the spectacular lobby. The giant light fixture sparkled high above us with what appeared to be large snowflakes. Our shoes and boots clipped across the marble floor.

Taking off my gloves with my satchel over my shoulder, we made our way to the front desk. It didn't take long before we were on our way up to our suite with a promise that our luggage would soon follow.

Once inside the Terrace suite, my eyes opened wide as I took in our new surroundings. From the living room with a fireplace, to a full kitchen, and two master bedrooms, there was easily as much space as my college apartment if not more. "Van, this is beautiful."

He led me to the windows in the living room, pulled back the curtains and revealed French doors. "A balcony. I know asking you to leave all of this behind and move to Northern Wisconsin is a lot. I thought while we were here, you should be in the heart of the city."

I laughed. "It's below freezing out there."

"Warmer than Ashland."

Lifting my arms around his neck, I brushed my lips over his. "I don't mind leaving this behind. I was actually dreading coming here."

"I knew that too."

"How did you get so intuitive, Mr. Sherman?"

"Let's just say I have years of practice at screwing up. Knowing what not to do is a good guide for learning what to do."

Taking a step back, I began to unbutton my coat as I stared out at the Gold Coast of Chicago. My thoughts centered on how in a short time everything had changed. Less than two weeks ago, I thought my life was all planned out and now...

When I turned toward Van, his topcoat and suit jacket were lying on a chair and his gaze was fixed on me. "What are you thinking?" I asked as anticipation sparked to life within me.

"I'm thinking I want to see the lace panties beneath those black slacks."

"If you're asking me to strip again for you, I think we should wait until our luggage is delivered. I don't want to be interrupted."

Van's smile grew as the golden flecks in his green orbs shimmered. "You're quite right again." He sighed. "It's more than luggage. There'll be a team here in a bit to make a few requested changes."

"Changes? Why?"

"We don't need two bedrooms. I need an office and so do you."

I spun around. "I can use the dining room table."

"You only have your laptop, same as I do. One bedroom will become an office and we'll both have extra monitors as well as a scanner, printer, and a few other necessities."

I shook my head. "I didn't know you could do that."

"Oh, beautiful, you can do anything for a price. There really is no limit."

"Like sabotaging the Sinclair-Wade merger?"

Van reached for my waist, his warm hold pulling me closer. "Don't be upset."

"I'm not. I want a chance to help Wade without losing it. That's what a merger would do. Wade would lose its identity." I looked up at him. "How much has this cost you?"

"That's insignificant."

"It's not. The balloon payment and now an investment in Sinclair."

Van shrugged. "Sinclair isn't a bad investment. They're farther in their trials for the PTSD drug than Wade is in their Alzheimer compound. I want to read more about Sinclair's research."

"Sinclair wasn't a questionable investment, but Wade was," I said, not asking.

His finger and thumb gently pinched my chin, bringing my gaze to his. "Yes, on paper. However, I have all the faith in the world in Wade's up-and-coming CEO. I hear she's a very quick learner."

I pressed against him. "Who told you that?"

"I have to keep the identity of my sources secret."

"No, Van. No secrets. I've told you more about me in a short time, things that even I didn't know. That's what you do to me. I feel open with you in a way I've never known. I want you open with me. I promise you won't scare me away."

His palm gently framed my cheek. "Time, Julia. This is new territory for me."

"I'll only give you until forever."

Van stepped back and reached for my coat. "I know we just got here, but let's get away while the crew is in the suite making the changes I've requested. We can get lunch and I have another idea."

"What idea?"

He pulled his phone from his pocket and sent a text message.

"What idea?" I repeated.

"I'm taking this opportunity, Julia." He offered me his hand. "Come with me?"

"Always."

Chapter 14

Van

As Julia and I settled in a back booth at a nearby restaurant, I found myself mesmerized by her smile. It did something to me, something I couldn't control—something I didn't want to control.

There were fires to tend, money to be made, and power to be claimed and yet, staring at the woman across from me—it was as if I were staring up at the sun. I basked in her warmth and was calmed by the tranquility of the sea of blue in her eyes.

Julia was freeing me from a prison of my own creation.

Brick by brick, she was knocking down the walls and bringing light to darkness.

She had no idea what she was doing or had done, the monster she'd awakened, or the sins that I'd committed. And yet she gave me the greatest gift, her willingness to wait. I could open up and unload the magnitude of my doings, but I feared that too much information too fast would scare her away.

I wouldn't let that happen.

I found her—finders keepers.

Julia was mine.

For once, my motivation wasn't completely self-serving.

While being with her fulfilled me, what I wanted above anything was to make her happy. I had other goals as well. I needed more.

More of her happiness.

More of her empowerment.

More of a world she desired.

Julia McGrath would find success in her own right. I'd facilitate it when I could, but above all, it would happen.

Julia looked around and after shrugging off her coat, she leaned across the table and spoke softly. "You continue to surprise me, Mr. Sherman."

"And how is that?"

"This is a burger place and a bar."

"Are you telling me that you don't eat burgers?"

She glanced down at the menu. "I mean, it's a common restaurant. With the Terrace suite at the Waldorf, I imagined dining on the famous French cuisine at Margeaux Brasserie."

"If that's your wish, we'll have dinner there."

She shook her head, soft blond curls framing her face as her cheeks rose and her perfect pink lips curled into a smile. "It's not. While I was raised with the advantages that money can buy, I don't need them." Her smile grew. "I have fabulous memories of a one-room cabin with no electricity, in the snow."

They say that opposites attract.

I reached across the table for her hands. "We'll go back to that one-room cabin and make more memories." I lifted her hand and lowered my lips to her knuckles. "Maybe it's because I wasn't raised with the finer things. I've worked for them, and I'm not satisfied. I want more."

"More and better," she replied. "Yet like here, you're comfortable with everyday pleasures."

"Oh, you see, that's where your lines have blurred. I'm looking at my everyday pleasure, and she is most definitely one of the finest things I've found."

A soft pink hue filled her cheeks as the waitress appeared at our table. "Welcome to Doc B's. I'm your waitress. What would you like to drink to start off your meal?"

Letting go of Julia's hands, I nodded across the table. "Ladies first."

"Water is fine for me."

When the waitress turned to me, I answered, "Coffee, black, and a glass of water."

Once she was gone, I sat taller, looking again around the restaurant, thankful that we'd missed the lunch crowd and were too early for the dinner crowd. "I'm not much for restaurants. I don't care for public exposure. However, breakfast was a long time ago, and I figured a burger joint was better than starving."

Julia looked up from the menu. "I forgot to be hungry when we were at Wade. Since you mentioned lunch, I've been famished."

"You truly were spectacular at Wade." I wasn't giving false praise. I didn't do that. Julia McGrath embodied the hope and idealism that had died within me until I found her along the side of the road. In the short time we'd been together, I was addicted to her vitality.

"I'm excited to get back to the suite and dive into the information."

I shook my head.

"What?"

"We have another stop after lunch."

She let out a long breath. "I could go back to the suite alone. The hotel isn't far away."

It wasn't.

We had walked from the hotel to the restaurant. Our next destination wasn't far either. A five- or six-minute walk, and I'd already prepared our security team. "I'm sure you're very capable alone on the streets of Chicago, but I want to keep you with me. We can walk."

"What are you planning?"

The waitress delivered our drinks, and we ordered our meals. Julia asked for a Chinese chicken salad, and I requested a Mediterranean shrimp salad. For a burger joint, they had an extensive menu.

Julia was placing the straw in her water glass when she asked again about where we needed to be.

"What if I want it to be a surprise?"

Her lower lip came forward in an adorable pout. "Then I'll obsess."

"You will?"

"Yes, I like surprises, and knowing one is coming will be all I think about."

I gave that some thought. "What if I told you that I have surprises planned for every night and every morning."

Julia's smile blossomed. "I like those surprises too."

"You may have an idea of what I have planned for the evenings and mornings, but I promise to keep you guessing."

I watched as her complexion filled with more pink, radiating from below her blouse, up her slender neck, and to her cheeks.

"Tell me what you're thinking," I whispered, my timbre filling my thoughts with possibilities. Though she didn't answer, my attention was drawn to the way her blouse tented with her hardening nipples.

Leaning forward, Julia giggled. "Stop that."

I lifted my brow in question. "I simply asked you a question."

"No, you have my thoughts going places that makes the need for food suddenly secondary."

"Good. Keep your thoughts there. Then when we get back to the suite, you'll be wet and ready."

"I already am." Her words were barely audible as she

looked down with her cheeks blushed and the waitress appeared with our food.

Despite Julia's comment about food being secondary, we both dug into our meals as our conversation waned. While I was anxious for our next destination, my mind went back to my meeting with Marlin.

He'd take the bait. I had no doubt.

Getting him out of Wade was not enough. Jeremy had provided me with an extensive list of both Marlin and Gwen's joint investments as well as Logan's portfolio, including information on offshore accounts that contained both common currency and cryptocurrency savings. My thoughts were a cyclone of ideas that would separate them from their money. I wouldn't be satisfied until their demise was both public and humiliating.

"I was obviously starving," Julia said, pulling me away from my thoughts.

The bowl before her was nearly as empty as mine.

"How well do your mother and Marlin get along?"

Julia shrugged. "I mean, Marlin is Dad's friend. Over time, the couples have gotten close. Mom and Gwen are better friends than Mom and Marlin." Her forehead furrowed. "Why?"

"Just curious." I looked at my watch. "We should move on soon. I'll flag down our waitress."

Reaching for her purse, Julia whispered. "I'll be right back."

"Don't be long."

For a moment, I enjoyed the sight of her walking

away. From the way her blond hair was pulled up and back, cascading in waves down her back, to her slender neck and proud shoulders, down her trim waist, and sexy round ass, Julia was a vision.

Before she disappeared around a corner, my gaze went to the bodyguard at the nearby booth. He nodded. As he stood to watch the bathroom, I reached for my phone and read the messages I'd missed during our lunch. The first text message was from Connie.

Mr. Sherman, your appointment is confirmed at Tiffany at three p.m.

I texted back.

You're a wonder. The suite is perfect. Remind me that you deserve a raise.

The other waiting text was from Lena.

Are you staying in Chicago long? Also, Jeremy has some interesting information for you—us. Call me when you can.

Did he have more information than what he'd sent earlier? My curiosity was piqued. I sent a quick reply.

Our schedule is up in the air. Still a long way from Montana.

That was Lena's current home base. She'd had enough of Chicago many years ago. She'd been in Washington state, delving in the world of computers and electronics. Montana was a recent move for her. Missoula, on the western edge of Montana, was a budding world of technology. It wasn't Silicone Valley yet, but it was quietly making a name for itself. Lena's investments included start-up companies that were making waves as well as cryptocurrency.

Lena replied.

Lucky for you, I'm not far away. Holidays, remember?

The coffee I'd just consumed left a sour taste as I responded.

Let me know if you're in the city. I'll check my schedule.

Her response was almost instantaneous.

(Laughing emoji) *You do that, Van. I'm more interested in Julia's schedule. Funny story. I remembered she and I have met. It's time to reminisce.*

My initial response was to ask about their meeting. My next was to tell Lena that Julia and I were leaving the city tonight. As I debated, out of the corner of my eye, I saw our waitress walk my way.

Choosing not to respond to Lena, I slid the phone back in my pocket as I handed the waitress my credit card, sipping the remaining contents of my coffee.

A few minutes later Julia returned.

She peered down at me, her head tilting. "Is everything all right?"

"As long as I have you."

Her blue eyes sparkled. "Only for forever."

Chapter 15

Julia

The sun streamed between the tall buildings as we walked south on Rush Street, my hand in Van's. The sidewalks were something I adored about Chicago. My picture had recently been on multiple news outlets. Donovan Sherman was a well-known businessman, and amongst the crowds of people we could be ourselves. People passed by completely lost in their own bubbles, unaware or uncaring of who was with them. There was a tranquilness in anonymity. For a few minutes among a crowd, we could simply be.

"I was wrong," I said as we passed Connors Park.

Van's cheeks had pinkened in the cool air. He turned to me, his green gaze drinking me in. "Tell me how you could be wrong."

"You told me this morning not to let Chicago bother me. I was. You knew that better than I did. And I was wrong." I lifted my chin to the cobalt-blue sky, feeling the cool breeze on my cheeks. "Chicago isn't bothersome. It's only a city."

"I lived here, long ago."

"You did? Where?"

"Not in the city. I lived west, near Schaumburg. I had an office in the city. My striving for more and better encouraged me to buy into the illusion that to be powerful you must be located in a big and powerful city."

Beneath the layers of coats and gloves, my skin electrified and my heart beat a steady rhythm at hearing Van speak, sharing even a small part of his past. I supposed this was information I could find in my research but reading it in a document paled in comparison to his spontaneous willingness to confide in me. "Did you drive every day into the city or did you ride the train?"

He smiled. "I had a car, but most of the time, I rode the train. I wanted more, but I also understood that I was on a quest with a shoestring budget. The train had multiple benefits. I could do work during the commute. It's why if I lived here now, I'd have a driver. Too much time is wasted in traffic."

My thoughts went to his home. "You don't have a driver in Ashland."

Van's laugh came out in a vapor. "I like to drive." He tilted his head toward the street congested with cars. "That isn't driving. It's sitting."

"How long ago was this?"

Van exhaled as his lips came together. "Around twenty years ago."

Scoffing, I shook my head.

His tenor filled with amusement. "I suppose that would have made you four years old."

"Oh, you should have looked me up back then. I had the cutest pigtails."

"While I was obsessing with more, you were obsessing with...?" He left the question open-ended.

I hummed. "At four years old...let me think." It was impossible to be certain of anything when I was that young. But something from my childhood stood out. "I believe it was Belle. I also wanted to be Mulan. They're Disney princesses," I added for reference.

Van squeezed my hand, tugging me toward him. "I know who they are. My niece went through a Disney phase." He looked up at the sky and back. "I'm not that removed from pop culture." He grinned down at me. "I can see that combination of Belle and Mulan in you."

"You should have seen me running around with a shield and sword in a golden ballgown."

"And pigtails."

His laugh rumbled through me.

"That's you, Julia, to a T. You're strong and brave, willing to risk it all for your family while at the same time being beautiful and feminine."

"I also have the urge to climb the ladder in your library and break out in song."

"Now that I want to see."

We came to a stop at the corner of Rush and East Chicago Avenue.

"Are we close?"

"We're close. And our appointment is in ten minutes. We're also on time."

Turning again on Michigan Avenue, we made our way past Ralph Lauren. Van slowed as we approached Victoria's Secret.

"Are you serious?" I asked. "I have a suitcase full of lingerie that was apparently not a gift."

"No," he said with a grin. "Our appointment is up here on the right."

My feet stopped walking as I read the sign. "You want...we have an appointment..." The increase in my pulse aided in my words' inability to conjoin in a way that created a full sentence. "At...Tiffany's?"

"We do. And if you don't know why, I'll get down on one knee here on one of the busiest streets in Chicago and propose again."

"I told you that I didn't care about a ring."

"I do. I care about you and about a ring."

With my feet rooted to the sidewalk, I looked up at him. "You want the world to know I'm taken." It wasn't really a question. Maybe I'd been jaded by Skylar and the way he obsessed about my engagement ring. Sometimes it felt as though the large emerald cut diamond surrounded by a halo of more diamonds was more for him than for me. It was as if he'd given me a neon sign to wear, one marking me as his.

Van reached for both of my hands. "I'll admit I do want the world to know. I love you and when any other man sees you, I want him to keep the fuck away. I also want a ring that's special to you. I want a ring that when you look at it, you don't see a sign saying you're a man's possession, but you see a ring that says you're loved and adored. I want a ring that brings you happiness by simply being upon your finger."

With a knot forming in my throat, I nodded. "Do you mind if it isn't huge?"

"I was thinking only six or seven carats."

Feeling the blood drain from my cheeks, I hoped he was joking. "I didn't pick out my ring from Skylar. He and his mom did." I shook my head, remembering the last time I saw it sitting on the countertop. "Sometimes when I'd put it on, I imagined a weight, one holding me down and back."

Van stood taller. "I want the opposite of that for you. I didn't know that you hadn't helped pick out the other ring, but now this is even more important. Will you please come inside and work with me and with the jeweler to find or create a ring that you will love and will wear, knowing that the last thing I want to do is hold you back? I want you to fly, Julia; I simply want to be there to help spread your wings."

He was doing what he did, listening, and somehow —with only words and his sexy green stare—not dismissing my concerns but addressing them head-on.

Nodding, I pushed to my tiptoes and brushed his cool lips with a kiss. "You make everything better."

He offered me his arm. "Come, Ms. McGrath, accompany me to find the ring of your dreams."

I placed my hand on his arm. "I'd be delighted."

A well-dressed woman met us at the door. "Ms. McGrath?"

"Yes," I answered, a bit surprised she hadn't addressed Van. "I'm Julia McGrath."

"I'm Gloria and we're so happy you chose to meet with us today."

My gaze darted between her and Van. "This is my fiancé, Donovan Sherman."

She winked my direction. "We can bring him along if you want."

"I do. I want him there."

"Please follow me," Gloria said as she led us past cases of stunning jewelry, diamonds, sapphires, rubies, and more. Finally, we came to an archway. "We have a fully stocked bar if you'd like a drink while we chat."

I was about to mention that it was three in the afternoon, but before I could, Van replied.

"I believe this monumental occasion calls for champagne."

"Yes," Gloria replied excitedly. "You're right." She lowered her voice, whispering to me. "You were right to invite him. He has good ideas."

I smiled at Van. "Yes, he does."

"We have our signature Hennessy champagnes. Moët or Dom Perignon?"

Nearly an hour later, sitting in a room with a long table, learning and exploring the four c's of diamonds—color, cut, clarity, and carat—and drinking more than one flute of Dom Perignon, I stared down at what was quite possibly the parts to the perfect ring.

"You have classic taste," Gloria said.

At no time had we discussed price.

I held the loose diamond in my fingers, taking in the two-and-a-half-carat round brilliant cut. Upon the platinum band was their signature Tiffany setting with six prongs. The color of the diamond was white, and the clarity was flawless.

It was simple and elegant.

"Will it weigh you down?" Van asked.

Tears came to my eyes as I shook my head. "It will help me remember that I'm loved. It will remind me to fly and to be the calm in a storm." I reached for his cheek and kissed him. For that moment, I didn't care that we were in a jewelry store or that Gloria was across the table from us. All that I cared about was the feeling that came to life within me, all because of the man at my side.

Gloria waited for our kiss to end. "It appears, Julia"—we'd moved onto a first-name basis between flute two and three— "that we have a winner."

"How soon can it be ready?" Van asked.

Gloria looked at the screen of her phone. "We will have the ring exactly to your specifications, size, and the matching wedding band by Friday afternoon."

When Van's green gaze came to mine, I nodded. "It's perfect."

"It seems we've made our decision," Van said.

I wasn't sure if it was the champagne or the ring or if it was just the way I felt special when I was with Van, but the walk back to the hotel passed in a blur. At only nearly five in the evening, the sky had darkened and all around us white lights flickered in the trees. As we approached the hotel, within the center of the circular driveway was a giant tree all decorated with sparkling lights.

Van stopped walking, still holding my hand. "Here's a tree for you, Julia. One decorated with lights." He kissed my lips. "One that shines but not as brilliantly as you."

It was a beautiful tree. I couldn't deny it.

"No, Van. My tree is in our cabin."

"*Our* cabin?"

I nodded. "I don't want to know if you were ever there with anyone else. All I need to know is that from now until forever, you'll only be there with me."

"That's a promise I never want to break."

Soon we were up in our suite as the lights of the city glowed beyond the windows. I wandered room by room, taking in the computer that was set up in the second master suite as well as the one on the dining room table. It was exactly what we needed to dig into work, yet it was the last thing I wanted to do.

"What are our plans for tonight?" I asked.

"We could get dressed up and go down to The Brasserie."

I laid my coat and gloves on a nearby chair and

tugged Van's topcoat off, leaving it with mine. After unbuttoning his suit coat, I wrapped my arms around his torso, pressed myself against him, and peered up through my lashes. "Is there a second option?"

His strong hands splayed over my behind, pulling me closer. In the few seconds that had passed, I felt the sensation of his erection against my stomach. His tenor lowered an octave. "We both do the work we missed."

I shook my head. "Option three."

"I turn on the fireplace, call for room service, and I spend the rest of the night taking you on every fucking surface in this suite."

The memories of us the first night in his house came back in a flood. I turned toward the tall windows, the ones with Chicago on the other side.

"Yes, Julia, I want you naked against the window with a whole city to watch as you come apart, squeezing my cock and screaming my name."

My insides twisted as I met his gaze. "I choose three."

Chapter 16

Julia

*W*earing only the robe with the hotel's monogram and sitting on the sofa in front of the fireplace, I reached for a piece of cheese from the tray filled with meats, cheeses, crackers, and jams. Before I had the chance to bring it to my lips, Van stole it from my grasp. His long fingers held tightly to the slice as he demanded my compliance.

"Open those luscious lips."

Despite the earlier sex, the timbre of his tone, mixed with his intense stare, created a delectable concoction that twisted my core and made me want more of what we'd already done. Instead of replying verbally, I did as he said, opening my lips and accepting the creamy cheese.

There was no concern that we would go hungry. I hadn't heard or seen when Van ordered our meal, but I was present when it arrived. One hotel employee after another wheeled linen-draped carts into the suite. Bottles of wine—yes, plural—and bottles of still water came first. The next cart was devoted to charcuterie selections and flatbreads. The third cart held two complete meals, one of roasted chicken and the other halibut and lentils. My eyes grew wide at the final cart with cheesecake, tarts, and brownies.

After the hotel employees left us alone, I shook my head. "Are you hungry?"

"No, beautiful. You will be. You'll need your strength for what I have planned."

That was nearly two hours ago and we'd yet to remove the silver domes from the main course.

After I swallowed the cheese, Van brought the rim of a wine glass to my lips. Unlike our holiday dinner, my hands weren't bound by a visible binding. Instead, they were immobile because of Van's commands, his encouragement, and his direction.

For a man who encouraged, supported, and helped me spread my wings and fly in everyday life, he was the polar opposite when it came to intimacy. That wasn't to say he wasn't encouraging and supportive. It was that in all things, he was in control.

His dominance came through in both his tone and his words. His commands reigned supreme in the sexiest of ways. All it took was a look or a change in his tone and I became putty, ready and willing to be formed into whatever Van desired.

Setting the wine glass on the nearby table and with only slight pressure from his fingers, Van laid me back on the soft sofa. The fire's flames reflected in his stare as he untied the sash and opened my robe. Inch by inch his sizzling gaze scanned my nakedness, lingering so long that my nipples again beaded, becoming hard as diamonds without a word or a touch.

That was what he did to me.

"You're fucking gorgeous." His green orbs met mine. "You know that, don't you?"

I shrugged. "I know that I'm glad you think I am."

"I don't think, Julia, I unequivocally know." As he spoke, he lifted one of my legs to the back of the sofa, opening me to him.

There wasn't any shame or even embarrassment on my part as he stared at my core, undoubtedly pink and wet from our earlier intercourse. I'd never imagined that I'd be this comfortable with a man, and yet with Van I was. It was as his touch moved slowly from my ankle to my inner thigh that I squirmed.

"Your pussy is perfection."

My flesh peppered with goose bumps as Van leaned forward, adding kisses, licks, and nips to his current chosen form of torture.

That was what it was, torture, as he teased and taunted.

My back arched and unrecognizable sounds filled the suite as he worked me with his fingers, lips, tongue, and teeth. I was a bundle of nerves, ready to explode as he successfully avoided where I needed him most.

With each encounter I'd learned that I was basically helpless in Van's hands.

I was an oarless boat being tossed at sea as wave

after wave of sensations washed over me. I reminded myself to float and enjoy the journey, and yet as his patience continued, mine would fade until my lips betrayed me, asking—begging—for relief.

"Open your eyes, Julia."

In the light from the flames, Donovan Sherman took my breath away. Statues of Greek gods paled in comparison. With his robe also gone, he was the definition of masculinity. All the stories I'd read and movies I'd seen created an ideal of what a man should be. That model seemed unattainable in any man I knew...until now.

The man standing above me was the epitome of those ideals.

Van offered me his hand.

Can I refuse?

I could.

Knowing that truth made acquiescing all the sweeter.

My hand appeared small as his fingers encased it, helping me from the sofa. All at once, Van was with me, against me, surrounding me. His hands on my hips. His lips on mine. We were moving, dancing a dance to the tune of the crackling fire. It didn't matter if I was unfamiliar with the steps. Van was the choreographer and master dancer. My pleasure and my reward would come by allowing him to lead.

Back and back, we stepped across the expanse of the living room.

My shoulders collided with the cool glass pane a second before I was spun around. My hands reached out, my fingers splaying on the window as stories below, the city was alive with people. We weren't isolated on Van's property with no one else around for miles.

He gathered my long hair, pulling it over one shoulder as his lips found the sensitive area of my neck. His words came out with puffs of air, tickling my skin.

"Imagine that they can see you, beautiful. Imagine that all the people along the streets and those in their cars have a front-row seat. They see you now. They can't peel their eyes away. You're too fucking stunning, a goddess. They're watching you, the way you move and the expressions you make. You're so damn receptive and they're drawn to you."

His words tickled my skin while their meanings reverberated within me, deep inside me, making my breasts heavy as my nipples became painfully hard. Van's erection prodded against me, but not where I wanted.

"What are they going to see?" he asked.

My mind was a mix of wanton need and overstimulation. It was crazy because he still wasn't really touching me, and yet I felt him everywhere.

I tried to form words. "Me...us. They'll see us."

Gently kicking the inside of my ankles, Van began the sculpting process, molding me to what he wanted and what would bring me the ultimate pleasure. The idea to fight it didn't even cross my mind. Soon I was leaning forward, my hands on the cool panes with circles of steam forming around them

My neck stretched as his cock teased my entrance.

I was wet, there was no need for him to check, yet he did. One and then two fingers. His rhythm lulled me into the misperception that I could anticipate his next move. I couldn't. I wouldn't. I called out as he brought my essence to my other virgin territory. The shock clouded my ability to protest as one finger pushed through, breaching what had never even been touched.

"Relax." His tone was soft, comforting. "I promise to make it feel good."

There was part of me that wanted to be embarrassed that Van would touch me there. As that thought came, the pleasure built. The man working me was an artist at his craft. While he continued the push and pull within my tight ring of muscles, he also tended to me, circling my clit, taunting my core.

The orgasm hit with absolutely no preamble. A defying thunderclap as lightning struck. My hands slid on the glass as I screamed his name and other less distinguishable sounds. My entire body trembled as Van stopped his torment and thrust inside me.

Despite the off-the-charts orgasm still ricocheting through my nerve endings, my core clenched around him with need. Panting for breath, my forehead fell to the window as I found his new rhythm. It was the dance with which I was becoming intimately familiar.

When I looked up, the window was covered in steam.

How can it not?

The heat we created was tropical despite the temperatures outside.

Van's thrusts came faster as his breathing quickened.

Through the steam or maybe because of it, I saw our reflection, muted as if someone had faded the scene. Holding my breath, I watched Van's face, wondering if the people below could see his masculine beauty, the way his neck strained and how the tendons and muscles pulled tight. Or if they could witness the rugged expression of pure bliss as he took what I willingly gave.

I was so enthralled with watching that I was caught off guard as a new orgasm began to build. Unlike the one before, this one came on slowly, inching its way through my circulation, a slow and steady train, as nerve endings sparked and synapses fired.

As the pressure mounted, I wiped away the steam and splayed my fingers as we both came undone.

Van's name echoed through the suite accompanied by his guttural roar.

His fingers held tight to my hips, pulling me to him and holding me tight.

My eyes closed as my back arched. Within me, his cock pulsated as my core clenched tighter and tighter. Words and curses came from behind me as his orgasm continued. Finally, the warmth and weight of his body curled over mine as Van's arms encircled my waist.

His deep baritone whisper taunted my perspiration-coated skin. "Julia, you leave me speechless. No word can describe what it's like to be with you. Phenomenal or fantastic doesn't even scratch the surface."

For a moment, we stayed with our union secure. In that time the world beyond the windows was forgotten, insignificant, as our togetherness grew stronger.

When Van stood straighter, our connection ended. He gently turned me until we were face-to-face. "Why did you wipe the window?"

"I didn't want all those people to miss the best part."

His lips quirked into a grin as his forehead came to mine. "The best part is you."

17

y pulse quickened as the raised voices came into range. A cyclone of thoughts ran through my brain at sonic speed, the most pressing being, What the fuck was happening?

As I pushed the key into the lock on my apartment door, I chastised myself for still living here, for putting Madison and Lena in danger. The volume of their voices exploded as the door swung inward. The entryway was as it had been when I left for the office this morning. The table and mirror were in place. I moved slowly, hoping to surprise whoever was here.

Butler. That was my first thought.

The fucker hadn't pressed charges when I beat the shit out of him. It was more than likely because my attorneys contacted him first. The agreed-upon mutual decision was that if Butler didn't want his ass in court as the defendant in a case charging him with domestic violence and the purchase of sexual services—not something that bodes well for him as an attorney himself—

and also as a witness in a second case against Infidelity, the piece-of-shit company that employed Lena and let her contract be bought out by Butler, then he'd keep his mouth shut about the beating I gave him.

Who was with Lena and Madison?

They were the only voices I heard above the roar of my blood circulating in my ears as I crept closer to the kitchen, near the back of the apartment.

I fucking needed a gun.

Why didn't I own a gun?

Then I remembered Lena's gun.

Did she have it?

Lena was the first to come into view. I moved closer, using to my advantage the element of surprise. "What the hell?"

My gaze darted between the two women. No one else was present. Both of their eyes grew large, probably thinking I'd lost my fucking mind.

"Van," they both said in unison.

"Holy fuck, I could hear you from the hallway. What the hell is going on?"

Madison crossed her arms over her breasts and tightened her jaw. "I'm sick and tired of being held prisoner in this apartment."

"You're not a prisoner," Lena replied. "It's for your—"

"Own good," Madison interrupted, her arms flying high before falling as she slapped her thighs.

Admittedly, I was having trouble shifting from

emergency alert to following this ridiculous and loud conversation. "Wait." I lifted my hand. "Why is this World War III?"

"Madison wants..."

"I need freedom..."

They both spoke at the same time.

I shook my head. "First, the apartment is temporary. I've got a deal in the works. When it pans out, we're going to have everything we want."

"What deal?" Lena asked.

"I just want to be free to work or shop or breathe," Madison added as she took a seat at the kitchen table.

"We need to get away from Chicago," I said. "Butler's too close and he knows where I live."

Lena turned to Madison. "Which is why you're not leaving the apartment."

"You both leave, every day."

My gaze met Lena's, silently saying that Madison was right. Lena and I both went out into the world. Even though her payment from Infidelity showed up in her bank account last month, she wasn't certain it would the next. There were still four more months on the contract, but she hadn't seen Nicholson or Butler since the night I brought her here.

In a nutshell, Lena was better equipped to be out in the world. Madison was...more delicate.

"What do you need?" I asked Madison. "We'll get it."

"This is ridiculous. You can't keep me from leaving."

"Fuck," Lena said, her voice filled with exasperation. "Logan threatened you. He's dangerous." Tears came to her light-brown eyes. "You saw what he did to me."

Madison reached out, laying her hand on her sister's arm. "I won't break."

Lena crouched down, next to Madison's chair. "You will. I told Mom and Dad that I'd take care of you. From the time they brought you home, I was told I was the big sister. It was my job to watch out for you." Her eyes met mine and went back to Madison. "I fucked up when I let Logan into our lives. I did that." Her volume rose. "I gave him access to our money and to us. I'll never forgive myself for that lapse in judgment. I swear on our parents' graves, I will make this all up to you. We're going to have it all back, twofold, tenfold."

It fucking killed me to watch the two of them. In the last year, they'd both become my family in all ways that mattered. It wasn't as if I had a relationship with my real family. I'd turned my back on them long before I got out of the hellhole in Texas. They'd made their choices. Olivia and Phillip may be able to forget what they did and the life they expected us to live, but I was done. Scrape the fucking shit off my boots and get out of Dodge.

"One day it will be us again," Lena said.

I didn't want it to be just them. I'd keep them both locked up and safe in this apartment or better yet, some fucking mansion, one away from neighbors, with a goddamned ten-foot-high perimeter if I could. The thing was that Lena was good and she was learning more about finance and investing. Hell, she had a backup plan, one she just revealed to me after I moved her in here.

Their conversation pulled me away from those thoughts.

"You don't owe me," Madison said. "I don't care about the money, and I'm not afraid of Logan. He's been nice to me."

Nice.

Not a word I'd use to describe him.

I guess that showed what a fucking great job Lena did at hiding shit from Madison.

"I'm not taking a chance," Lena said.

"Butler hasn't been around since that night," I said. "Maybe my attorneys scared him straight."

Madison grinned my direction, her green eyes shining. "And you told him we were married."

I lifted my chin toward her hand.

She looked down at the plain white-gold band and back to me. "It's dumb to wear this fake ring when I'm a prisoner in this place. I mean, who will see it?"

"Logan could show up," Lena said. "We have to be ready on all counts."

"Once this deal is complete, we'll move," I said, "away from the city."

Lena shrugged. "I'm still worried that I'll have to repay Infidelity. If I do" —she sighed— "we can't afford..."

"How is your side job coming?" I asked with a smile.

Her lips curled and her cheeks rose for the first time since I'd walked into this battle. "So far, so good."

"What side job?" Madison asked.

"Let's just say that Logan was a little too open with his passwords."

Madison's green stare widened. "You're stealing from him?"

"I consider it more like reimbursement for what he stole from us, a little at a time."

"Tell me, do we have money?"

Lena sighed. "What we have needs to last until it's beyond when Infidelity could ask me to pay them back. Once we make it beyond that, things will look up."

Madison turned toward me. "So I'm a prisoner waiting for your deal." She turned to Lena. "And your imaginary timeline."

When we didn't respond, Madison turned back to me. "I was talking to Olivia—"

My entire body stiffened at my sister's name. "Why would you do that?"

Madison stood and walked toward me. "Because I'm bored. Because she calls me."

I shook my head. "Fuck no. I've told you my family is—"

Her hands came to my chest. "You've said that Olivia is different. She cares about you, Van. You won't call her so I do."

My hands gripped her shoulders. "No more."

"We aren't really married. You can't tell me what to do."

"And even if you were..." Lena said from beyond our bubble as Madison rolled her eyes.

"She invited me down to San Antonio for a while. It will get me out of the house and Logan Butler won't have any idea where I am."

The idea of Madison being down there with my family made me physically ill. Olivia was one thing, but my parents and Lip would corrupt her, they'd tell her things, things she didn't need to know.

"It's not a bad idea," Lena said. "I like it better than your idea to get a job here around Chicago."

"It's a horrible idea," I said. "How about going back to taking art classes? You said you would consider that."

"I need a break," Madison said. "I'm sick of the tension around here. I'm sick of the talk of the future that will never come."

"It will come. One day we'll have it all. I'm going to make it big and when I do, I'll show you. I'll name my company after you."

"I don't want more. I just want a life."

Chapter 18

Julia
Present day

This was the third day I'd spent at the dining room table immersed in all things Wade Pharmaceutical. I'd awakened early and eased my way out of bed, making my way to the table before the sun rose. It was the first time I could recall waking before Van.

With my hair piled on top of my head in a messy bun, I was certain there was at least one or two pens buried in the mess—it could be more. The button-down shirt I wore as a dress had the long sleeves rolled up. The shirt was on its second day—first for me. Van wore it yesterday, and in the darkness of the bedroom, I couldn't resist gathering it from the floor while he slept. Every now and then, simply seeing it and catching the aroma of Van eased my mind.

Now, it was almost noon and despite the copious notes, I felt that I was no closer to understanding the information. Beside the large computer monitors Van had had delivered, I had two notebooks filled with notes, chicken scratch really, of points of interest and files I wanted to revisit.

The deeper I dove into the data, the more I realized that my last year working at Wade was for nothing more than show. I hadn't been a contributing employee. While I was guilty of not asking, I hadn't been given the tools to be useful.

As I sipped a new cup of coffee, I vowed that had changed. From this point on, my employment and involvement wouldn't be in name only.

Taking a deep breath, I lifted my arms over my head and stretched. As I did, strong hands came from behind me, fingers searched beneath the neck of the shirt, massaging my shoulders. Before I could comment or tell Van how good it felt, warm lips teased my exposed neck. Van's kisses were the epicenter as goose bumps scattered over my skin.

Surrounded in a cloud of Van's spicy aftershave, I turned, meeting his green stare as his deep voice rumbled through me.

"You haven't moved from this chair since before we had breakfast delivered."

"I know. I want to do my best."

"I have no doubt."

"I feel like there is something I need to find, something I should know. I feel like whatever it is it's right there. I just don't see it."

Van reached for my hand, his fingers surrounding

mine as he urged me to stand. "I was thinking it would be good for you to move around a bit."

My lips quirked to a grin. "Do you have any ideas how I could do that?"

"I have a lot of ideas." He teased a button from its hole. "Most of those ideas include losing my shirt."

I playfully pushed his hand away. "I like wearing your shirt."

"I like you wearing them. I like you wearing nothing even more."

It was at that moment I realized that unlike me, Van was not only showered and shaved, but he was also dressed in his suit, sans the suit coat and tie. I reached up to his collar. "You look very handsome. Are you going somewhere?"

He nodded as his forehead came to mine. "I've been avoiding someone who's also in town. And this afternoon, that's coming to an end."

"Avoiding? Why?"

"Someday, Julia, when we have a few days to spend uninterrupted, I'll tell you the whole story. Right now, it's an old friend who has information that can apparently only be shared with me in person."

I stood straighter, wondering if this old friend was male or female. I'd never been the jealous type. Then again, with my track record of what Skylar did to me, I should have asked more questions. "Should I be concerned that you're off to meet a beautiful woman?"

"Not in the least." He left a soft kiss on the end of

my nose. "I won't be gone long. I plan on being back to accompany my fiancée to her parents' home for New Year's Eve."

I shook my head. "I told Mom we couldn't attend. Besides, it will be formal attire, and my formal dresses are in my closet at their house, not here."

"I told Gregg we would be there."

Leaning against the dining room table, I crossed my arms over my breasts. "I know why you think we should go. I get it, the whole show-I'm-strong thing, but if I could have one New Year's Eve wish, it would be that it was only the two of us, in our cabin with a fire and what remains of our tree."

"We can do that. I will miss my meeting. You can leave all of this" —he gestured toward the table— "behind for a few days, and Ruth and Andrew can have the plane ready to leave in an hour."

"Do you know how tempting that is?"

"Say the word. Avoiding your parents' gathering would be much less complicated if we were in Ashland."

I lifted my palms to my temples. "I've been avoiding the thoughts, burying myself in the information from Wade, but tonight..." I didn't want to say the words.

"Was your wedding night."

I nodded, an unexpected pang of sadness settling in my chest. The emotion wasn't for the loss of the overly extravagant wedding and reception, or God forbid, the loss of Skylar Butler. And still, I didn't want to explore the feeling thoroughly enough to fully understand why it was there. Maybe it was simply the loss of every little girl's fairy tale.

The tale where your Prince Charming never lets you down.

Before I could explore those thoughts any longer, Van reached for my waist and lifted me to the edge of the table. Spreading my knees apart, he came closer, his fingers lifting my chin with his gaze fixed on mine. "It could be your wedding day. Plan B, I cancel my meeting and you and I go to the Cook County Clerk's Office or the Marriage Court and we make this legal." He looked down at his watch. "I'm not sure what time they close, but I could get Connie on it. I'm confident that an exception can be made."

My face tilted. "Do you, Mr. Sherman, hold that much power that you can dictate governmental offices hours?"

"The short answer is yes."

Having Van this close caused a visceral reaction—my skin to warm, my pulse to quicken, and my core to clench. It wasn't conscious and I couldn't control it, nor did I want to.

Red sin.

I closed my eyes, allowing myself to get lost in the sound of his deep, confident voice, the spiciness of his scent, the warmth of his touch, and the hum within me that his close proximity created.

"Open your eyes."

As if he had the magical power to make his words

the undeniable reality, my eyelids opened, adding to my sensory overload. Only inches away was his handsome face, mesmerizing gaze, and firm lips.

"You left the bed this morning before me."

The tenor of his tone caused my stomach to flip-flop and my core to tighten. Unconsciously, I tried to press my thighs together, but they were trapped with him in between. "I woke up and my mind was filled with bits and pieces."

Van's finger came to my lips. "You need to relax." His touch skirted up my bare legs, sending sensations throughout my circulation.

"Van," I panted. "You have a meeting."

He ran his finger over the cotton crotch of my lace panties as his smile grew. "My meeting can wait."

"I..." I started to say that I had work to do. However, before I could voice a protest, he pushed the cotton aside and ran his thumb over my clit, making circles as thoughts of Wade momentarily melted away. With his other hand, he unbuttoned the shirt, allowing it to fall open and leaving me mostly bare to him.

"Look at me, beautiful," he said as he tugged free one pen and then another I'd buried in my hair. As the long locks cascaded down my back, he added, "I want to have your come on my fingers and the vision of you coming apart when I leave."

I placed my arms behind me, thankful he'd set me to the side of the monitors. Biting my lower lip, I concentrated on the roaring fire in his gaze. The golden and green flames flickered and sparked, scorching my skin and searing my breasts as they grew heavy and my nipples drew taut.

I sucked in a breath as one and then two fingers plunged inside me while his thumb continued its caresses of my growingly sensitive clit. My hips bucked to the rhythm he created. The blaze in his green orbs grew to a raging fire as around us the room, the suite, the entire city, disappeared.

It was as he curled his fingers that I came undone.

My whole body tensed as sounds echoed from my lips to the walls of the suite.

As my core spasmed and shuddered around his long fingers, coating them with my essence, I fought to breathe, to fill my lungs. Van didn't stop, keeping me mesmerized by the intensity of his stare.

Free falling from high in the Chicago skyline, endorphins flooded my circulation, relaxing my muscles. It was as I was about to lie back on the table that Van wrapped his free arm around me and pulled me toward him.

"You're so fucking beautiful when you come." He shook his head before he lifted his fingers to his nose. "You smell sweet." Parting his firm lips, he sucked them. "And taste even better."

I shook my head in disbelief. "You're seriously going to your meeting like that?"

"I am."

"I guess I don't need to be worried that you're meeting some beautiful lady."

He let his forehead again fall to mine. "I'm with the most beautiful lady at this second."

As Van helped me from the table, I began to button the front of the shirt. My task was almost complete when he asked about my research. While I would have loved to float endlessly in the post-orgasmic bliss, I stared up at him, surprised and pleased with his interest. In all reality, I was also anxious for his opinion.

"I started thinking about the balloon payment."

"What about it?" He asked as he reached for a necktie lying over a chair.

I ran the fabric through my fingers. "Is that satin?"

Van's lips curled into a grin. "If we go down that road, we'll both be unavailable to have meetings or do work."

"Will I be tied up?" I asked with a bat of my eyelashes.

"You're playing with fire."

"I like fire."

"Oh, I promise a forest fire when I get back. First, tell me about your thoughts on the balloon payment."

As he tied his necktie and donned his suit coat, I told him what I'd been thinking. "It seems like it would take more than the cancellation of my wedding for a bank to demand such a high payment. I've been going through documents, wondering if the balloon payment was a condition of the original loan. So far, I haven't found anything, but if it was, Dad would have known it was coming."

Van stood straighter, looking all GQ, the complete opposite of my post-orgasmic mess. "And so did Butler."

I shrugged, gathering my hair back to the top of my head. "I really don't know what Skylar knew."

"Marlin. If he knew it was coming due the first of the year..." His words trailed away.

My eyes widened. "That's why he wanted to sell. If he had the shares by yesterday, he could have arranged a sale before Wade defaulted."

"It would have been tricky. He couldn't have let the prospective buyers know that the looming payment was coming. He was cutting it awfully short." Before I could respond, Van added, "Then again, the sale would satisfy the loan in its entirety and avoid the balloon payment."

"It would benefit him but would result in Wade being swallowed by Big Pharma."

"His plan would have ruined Wade, but all of the shareholders would benefit."

The thought churned the coffee in my stomach. "Even my parents."

Van nodded.

"I'm going to keep digging."

Van's palms came to my cheeks, lifting my face as his lips met mine. "For the record, I don't like waking without you."

Something with his tone reverberated through me. "Are you holding me captive in my bed?"

He shook his head. "Never. And also on the record" —he tilted his head toward the computer screens— "I'm fucking impressed. You were born for this. Don't ever let me or anyone keep you from following your gut."

"I wish my gut wasn't making me question my father."

"Keep digging and maybe it will clear him."

Pressing my lips together, I nodded.

"I love you," he said with another kiss. "And I won't be long. Your lunch will be arriving in an hour. I'd prefer if you didn't leave the suite. If you do, let me know." He stood straighter as a shadow passed through his eyes. "You're not captive, Julia."

A smile came to my lips. "I was joking."

"I've made enemies and right now, things are public with our engagement. It would be safer for you to stay here."

"I don't plan on going anywhere." I looked down at the shirt. "Besides, I'm not dressed."

He playfully tugged on a button. "You're too dressed."

Chapter 19

Van

On the way to my meeting, I sent Connie a text. It had to do with Julia's reasoning for not attending tonight's party.

I didn't blame Julia for her apprehension considering today was the date of her canceled wedding. If Connie could continue her magic, in a few hours Julia would receive a delivery, complete with everything she will need for tonight's party. Hell, Julia was gorgeous in my shirt, but for this occasion, she should not only feel beautiful but also powerful because that was what she was.

Though I'd been unable to get a complete confirmed copy of tonight's guestlist, it was safe to assume that Marlin, Gwen, and Skylar Butler would be in attendance. There was one other Butler I wondered about —Logan.

Michael pulled the sedan near the curb in front of the restaurant. "I'll be waiting for your call, Mr. Sherman."

"Thank you, Michael. Keep the man outside the

suite. I don't want Julia leaving, but if she does, I want her followed."

"Is there a particular threat? A person we should be watching for?"

Fuck, I wish I knew.

The list was growing by the moment.

My private detective had yet to locate Phillip. My brother's house was empty, a fact that now had me concerned about Brooklyn. I'd told the detective to check my parents' home in Austin. It was the holidays. Family gathers. That was the most reasonable explanation.

And also under the category of threats, there were the Butlers. Marlin was obviously displeased that I wouldn't play his game. Nevertheless, I didn't see him as the dangerous one, not in a physical sense of the word. Oh, he'd fuck Julia and me out of Wade and money if he could, but he wasn't the one who was prone to violence. That was Logan.

I answered Michael. "Ms. McGrath is to be my wife. That in and of itself is a threat."

"Yes, sir. We have one man watching the suite and another in the lobby ready to move if necessary."

"I gave her your cell-phone number. If she wants to go somewhere beyond walking distance, she agreed to call you."

"And if she does, I'll call you," he said.

I nodded as my phone vibrated. The text from Connie confirmed that her magical powers were still working. Julia would be getting a delivery from Saks Fifth Avenue this afternoon. Connie didn't elaborate more than that the dress and shoes would be perfect for Julia.

Michael came around, opened my door.

As a light flurry of snow swirled between the buildings, I stepped out onto the sidewalk and tugged at the sleeve of my topcoat as from the corner of North Rush Street and Grand Avenue, I looked up and down both streets.

"Sir, I can park the car and come inside."

"That won't be necessary. I can handle myself. It's Julia I'm concerned about."

It was probably being back in the city.

No matter the cause, I had an uneasy sensation I couldn't shake, like an itch that can't be scratched. Nothing significant, just infuriatingly irritating. I was fucking ready to get Julia back to our snow globe.

Entering Joe's Seafood on the Magnificent Mile, I took in the rich decor, the dark wood, and the ambience. I should be here with Julia. I wasn't. In no time at all, I spotted Lena at a table near the back of the room.

"May I help you?" the hostess asked.

Lena lifted her martini glass and grinned her painted smile.

"No, thank you. My party is here."

I made my way through the tables, taking in Lena's short hairstyle, the current shade was darker than before with more red. She was a beautiful woman and had gotten even prettier with time. It wasn't her shell alone that improved her appearance. It was the confidence that she possessed, the ingredient she lacked when we first met.

When I reached the table, Lena stood, leaned close, and placed her hand on my shoulder as she gave a chaste kiss to my cheek. Returning the gesture, I found myself surrounded by her perfume. It wasn't too much, but I knew from experience that it was expensive. The classic scent was part of her signature, the blended mix of flowers, fruits, and spices. Creed Royal Service and Lena went hand in hand.

"Van, I'm glad you could fit me into your busy schedule."

"Lena, always a pleasure."

She made a show of peering behind me. "Where is your fiancée?"

Shaking my head, I draped my overcoat on the back of the chair, unbuttoned my suit coat, and took my seat in the chair opposite her. A quick scratch of my nose and my smile materialized. I'd take the scent of my fingers over a two-thousand-dollar bottle of perfume any day.

Lena lifted the glass. "You really should try their lemon drop martini. After all, it's New Year's Eve." Her soft-brown eyes went to the window. "It's guaranteed to warm you up on a day like today."

"Sir," a young woman said, appearing at our table,

"may I get you something to drink while you look at our menu?"

"Coffee, black."

Lena's painted lips curled into a smile as the waitress walked away. "Always such a fuddy-duddy." She leaned forward. "You have heard that all work and no play makes Van a dull man?"

Not looking at the menu and placing it on the table, I also sat forward. "Did you get an inquiry from Marlin?"

"Aphrodite Corporation has been contacted."

"GreenSphere?"

"I've made some headway," she said.

"They contacted you with only a five-share investment, and yet I haven't been contacted with twenty-six."

"I still don't know who the mysterious investors are," Lena admitted. "Jeremy and his team are digging. Whoever controls GreenSphere has gone to a lot of trouble to keep it private. They secured the two shares from Wolfe."

I sat back, shaking my head. "Fuck, when?"

She tilted her chin toward her phone. "It would've had to have been yesterday, but Jeremy just sent me the information."

Removing my phone from my inside suit coat pocket, I saw one text from Jeremy. "The GreenSphere thing has me baffled. I have people digging too." When her eyes widened, I added, "Nothing. They're meeting the same roadblocks."

"Here's my proposal. We—you and Aphrodite—unite under one umbrella. It'll make us a more formidable opponent."

I shook my head. "The shares of Wade I acquired are for Julia, not for me. I can't."

"Together we'd have thirty-one. And if we could become investors in GreenSphere, we'd have a portion of their five."

The waitress delivered my coffee. Before she could ask if we were ready to order, both Lena and I shook our head, essentially waving her away.

I voiced a concern that had been milling around in my thoughts. "Why does some multi-million-dollar SPAC want five measly percent of shares in a small private pharmaceutical company?"

"You sparked the interest." Her smile grew. "The reclusive wolf of high finance not only swooped in to save a struggling company but shocked the world with the news of his engagement to the Wade Pharmaceutical heiress. And here I thought you were a committed bachelor for life." She lifted her glass to her lips. "Apparently what you were looking for was a princess whose kingdom was about to fall."

"I wasn't looking. You above anyone should know that."

"I do know and hindsight improves everyone's vision. You weren't the only one who made poor choices. You've punished yourself long enough, Van. Live before it's too late."

"That sounds like your blessing, Lena."

She shrugged. "We deserve to have it all, you and me."

Inhaling, I fought the urge to ask about Madison.

Meeting with Lena wasn't in any way being unfaithful to Julia. There was nothing about the woman across the table that could arouse my sexual interest. She was a good fuck and so was I, but that was all it had ever been. No, Lena was my friend and my sometimes partner in business, revenge, and destruction. Asking about her sister would be crossing a line I wouldn't cross.

Julia deserved the new and improved Donovan Sherman.

Keeping that forefront in my mind wasn't easy, but another scratch of my nose reminded me that being a better man for Julia also wasn't difficult. Julia was hardly a consolation prize. She was the top of the top. The star at the top of the fucking tree. I didn't deserve her, but that wouldn't stop me from never letting her go.

"She is it," I said. "She's the all that I didn't realize was missing."

Lena lifted her martini glass with a sly smile. "It's nice not being the ones seeing the green."

"I haven't given it much thought."

She lifted her chin and looked around the expensive restaurant. "I think it's being back in this city. I remember what it was like." She offered her glass in a cheers gesture.

I lifted my coffee cup.

"We've done it, Van. Now they look at us with envy, not the other way around."

"I wasn't looking for Julia," I said again, "but I found her." My lips quirked upward. "Literally found her."

"Was she lost?"

"What you just said is correct. Finding her made me realize, it's been me. I was lost. I have been. And her connection to Wade Pharmaceutical reminded me about a fight I never finished."

"We," Lena corrected.

"That's why I'm here. I owe you."

She pushed a napkin my direction. "May I get that in writing, Van? Be sure to add lots of zeros after whatever you say I'm owed."

"Are napkin contracts now legally binding?"

The waitress appeared again.

Lena opened the menu and pointed. "We both want this."

"To share?"

Lena's brown orbs looked up through her extra-long lashes.

I reached over and closed the menu. "Make it two. I'm too hungry to share." The innuendos may have gone over the waitress's head, but Lena and I were well aware of the subconversation occurring. My response wasn't for the waitress. Once she left, I asked, "What did we order?"

Lena shook her head as the ends of her auburn hair teased her shoulders. "I don't know."

"Did Aphrodite make Marlin an offer?"

"Not yet. I have a message out to GreenSphere. Marlin may think he can go shareholder to shareholder to get his price up. With Wolfe no longer in the picture, we have to unite and sabotage his plan."

I nodded. "Jeremy sent me a comprehensive list of Marlin and Gwen's investments. He's toying in crypto."

"Isn't everyone? It was the offshore accounts that had my attention." She tilted her head. "Surely you didn't think Jeremy would only share with you."

Share.

"I'm not surprised." I leaned forward again. "Allotting information is as far as our sharing is going to go. Tell me when you met Julia."

"Are you sure she's not willing—to share? You know this younger generation is progressive in their thinking. You won't know if you don't ask."

I lifted my brows and spaced my words. "I. Won't. Share."

"I see, so you haven't asked." Lena pursed her lips and shook her head. "This is where you get yourself into trouble. You need to watch that selfish tendency."

Swallowing, I let out a breath. "The two of you met?"

"Years ago. I doubt she remembers. It was with

Logan, before I knew you. As he was originally screwing us over and before I saw him for who he is. It was Thanksgiving or some occasion. As I recall, Skylar and Julia were children...young children."

"Julia tells me she had cute pigtails."

Lena laughed. "I don't recall. Kids were never my thing."

"She's no longer a child."

The waitress arrived, plates in hand. Two servings of seared ahi tuna salad with slivered peanuts were placed before us. "More coffee, sir?"

"Yes, and" —I opened my eyes wide— "does the lady need another martini?"

"I'm fine with my water. I need to pace myself. Tonight is New Year's Eve."

Once we were alone, I looked at our meals. "It's fortunate that neither of us is allergic to peanuts or seafood."

"We aren't. I'm most positive I know all your secrets."

"And I yours." I took a bite. "This is good."

"For what you're paying, it should be."

I scoffed and told Lena what was on my mind. "I can't find Phillip."

"Maybe he's lost like you were."

"I'm serious, Lena. He's called Connie multiple times, yelling at her and demanding to talk to me or Julia and now he's MIA."

"All I know is that he'd been in contact with Logan

or vice versa."

"What about Brooklyn?"

Lena laid her fork down and exhaled. "Van, you agreed..."

My voice lowered to a whispered growl. "I'm not fucking near her. I want to know that she's all right."

"She's staying with Olivia. I only know that because I received postal notice that Brooklyn's gift was forwarded. The address where it was sent is your sister's."

Chapter 20

Julia

When I heard the knock at the door, I assumed it was an employee of the hotel coming to pick up the room-service cart from lunch. Imagine my surprise when it was a delivery. The man entering laid a long garment bag and a large black and white striped bag on the sofa.

"Are you sure you're delivering this to the correct room number?"

He looked at a slip of paper. "Ms. McGrath, the Terrace suite."

"That's me," I said, warmth filling my cheeks at the realization I was still wearing Van's shirt. "Oh, let me get you a tip."

Hurrying to the bedroom, I found my purse and returned with a twenty-dollar bill.

"Thank you, ma'am."

Once he was gone and the door was locked, I went to the sofa, curiosity getting the better of me. Unzipping the long bag, I gasped. It was an evening gown, a stunning red, bright red, cherry red gown.

"Damn you, Van," I muttered as I pulled it from the bag.

There went my excuse for not attending tonight's party.

I ran my fingers over the fine fabric, noticing the long cape sleeves. The tag said Safiyaa. Draping the gown over the sofa, I went to the Saks Fifth Avenue bag and discovered matching red shoes—Jimmy Choo patent leather with a rhinestone embellished strap.

If Van's intention was to make me the center of attention, this would do it.

I'd been so lost in the Wade information that I'd lost track of time. A quick look out the tall windows told me that the sun was starting to set. Van had said he wouldn't be long, but at least three hours had passed. I looked at my phone, hoping for a message.

As I was about to text him, the door sounded with the noises of it unlocking.

Placing my fists on my hips, I did my best to look mad.

All it took was his gaze going from me to the couch and back to me and the sight of his smile to wear down my pretend anger. "I still don't want to go."

Laying his wool coat over a chair, he came my way. His hands gripped my waist as he pulled my hips to his. "What if I promise to make it up to you?"

"Cocktails are at seven. You could make it up to me now."

"I like the way you think."

Starting near the top, Van began undoing the buttons of the shirt I wore.

"Do I smell perfume?" I asked, a bit taken aback.

"You may." His fingers continued their mission.

I took a step away from him. "I'm not the jealous type, Van, and that screwed me with Skylar."

"The only screwing you got."

My fists returned to my hips. "Your meeting. It was with a woman." I wasn't asking.

"Yes, it was. As I said, when you and I have the time, I will explain. Lena is an old friend. We've been in business off and on together over the years. She lives in Montana. I live in Ashland. Even though we were both in Chicago, I'd avoided seeing her, but as I said earlier, meeting with her couldn't be completely avoided."

"And you were with her for over three hours." I didn't care if I sounded jealous. I was distracted by the new cracks forming in our snow globe.

The shirt was nearly unbuttoned as Van stepped closer. "No. We met for lunch at Joe's Seafood. After lunch, she went her way, and I went mine. There was an unfinished matter. Since I was out, I thought I'd tend to it myself."

"What?"

"You know that I love you," he said.

I shook my head. "I'm sorry. I just can't be cheated on, not again."

"I'd never do that."

Looking up through my lashes, I asked, "What was your errand?"

Van reached for my hand, led me to a soft chair, and encouraged me to sit. Crouching near my knees, that I had pressed together, Van looked up at me. His green orbs sparked as they scanned from my lace panties to my breasts and finally to my eyes.

"Fidelity is never an issue, Julia. You're mine. I'm yours. Our relationship has taken off at cosmic speed, but that doesn't lessen its sincerity. When I'm with you, it's as if we've always been meant for one another." He reached out, touching my hair, pulling a pen from the bun and loosening the tie. Skirting my locks over my shoulders, he grinned. "The problem was that when I was younger, I didn't deserve you. I still don't. When you were in pigtails, I was fucking up. I did it very well. That's why we're so right for one another. I've learned from my mistakes, and I know with all my heart that being the best man I can be for you and with you is what you deserve."

I swallowed the lump forming in my throat. "I'm sorry." My palm gently came to his cheek. "You are the man I deserve. I feel your goodness. Your encouragement has been more than I've ever had, and I hope that you feel my gratitude and my love in return."

Van reached into his suit coat pocket and pulled out a small velvet box.

"Oh." My vision blurred. "You picked up my ring."

He opened the box, showing me three rings.

It wasn't the large diamond that I picked up. It was the thick round band. I turned it around in my fingers. Finally, my gaze met his. "You got our wedding bands, one for you too."

Van nodded. "I want you to wear my ring to remind you every minute that you're loved, that I'm so fucking impressed with you, and that I'll be with you and encouraging you to spread your wings and fly." He took his ring from me. "I want to wear this ring after we say our vows for the same reason. I want to look at it and sense your love. I want to wear it, so the world knows that I too am taken. There's only one woman in my life, Julia, and you're her."

He put his ring back into the box and removed the engagement ring. "I'd planned to give this to you right before we left for your parents', but now is as good of a time as any."

I spread out my fingers on my left hand, allowing Van to gently tease the platinum band and diamond over my knuckle. As he did, something within my chest burst, filling me with hope in a way I'd never before experienced.

My arms went around his neck, pulling me to him.

"Are you done" —he tilted his chin toward the dining room— "for today?"

I nodded. "I think I'd rather do something else."

"Cocktails at seven?" he asked.

"There is something I was wondering if you could help with?"

Van stood, taking my hand and encouraging me to stand. "Something with the information on Wade?"

I looked down at the gorgeous ring and wiggled my finger, noticing the way the diamond sparkled under the overhead lighting. When I looked back, I grinned. "As you know, I don't want to attend my parents' gala."

"You have mentioned that."

"I will. I mean you bought me clothes and now I have the ring..." I undid his tie, pulling the material from the knot.

"Is there something else?"

I freed the necktie from his collar. "Well, Mr. Sherman, I'm afraid that I'm sounding needy. You've done so much already."

"My curiosity is piqued. Tell me what you want, Julia, and if it's within my power, I will do it."

Handing him his necktie, I said, "I want to enter the party freshly fucked."

Van's eyes opened wide as a chuckle came from his throat. "I can help with that."

Our fingers intertwined. "I thought you could."

"Only thought? I'll have to prove it."

"Lead the way," I said with a grin, knowing that was exactly what he would do.

Standing at the full-length mirror in the bedroom, I looked into the reflection at the man behind me. He was absolutely panty-melting in his custom suit and a new tie, one that matched my red dress. It had been in the Saks Fifth Avenue bag. Understandably, my attention had been drawn to the high-heeled shoes I now wore.

My hair was fashioned up in a much more stylish hairdo than my earlier messy bun. I was freshly showered and freshly fucked—not completely in that order. Neither of those points may be obvious to anyone else at my parents' party but I didn't care. I knew them and so did Van.

His gaze met mine in the mirror as he zipped the back of the gown. "You are a vision, Julia. I look forward to unzipping this later tonight."

"I'm going to make you wait until next year before you can do that."

He kissed my neck. "It will be worth the wait." Van reached for my left hand. It wasn't the ring he was inspecting but my wrist.

"I told you that satin was more forgiving."

"I don't deserve you."

I spun until I was facing him. "I do love you, Van. I want everyone to know that." Before he could respond, I added, "Kiss me before I put on lipstick."

"Yes, ma'am."

My eyes closed as his embrace encircled me, pulling my breasts against his solid chest. Even though I would rather be in our cabin, I knew I could attend this gathering for one reason—because of the man at my side.

He continued to tell me how strong I am, but I know it's not all me. It's what Van does to me and how he has empowered me in a way that never existed.

After Van contacted Michael, the driver who he'd apparently hired for our indefinite stay, he asked, "Did you learn anything about the balloon payment?"

"I did."

"You did?"

"I think it's important. Later, will you look at a correspondence chain I found? I'd like your opinion."

"Correspondence between whom?" Van asked.

"A bank officer assigned to Wade's account."

"And Marlin?"

I shook my head, the answer adding to my unease about tonight's gathering. "My mom."

Chapter 21

Julia

*V*an held tightly to my hand as we sat in the back seat, and Michael slowly progressed, moving us forward in a line of cars waiting to enter the rounded brick driveway leading to my parents' home. Nestled in Lincoln Park, our family home was one of the neighborhood's treasures. That was a direct quote from my mother.

The limestone residence was purchased by my grandparents, Herman and Juliette Wade. This New Year's Eve event was an annual tradition. Of course, this year, it was supposed to take place downtown, following my wedding.

I pushed those thoughts away. As my gaze went to the white lights twinkling in the trees and glistening in the cold air, I had a thought. Speaking softly, I whispered, "My parents inherited this house from my grandfather Herman."

"It's not Buckingham Palace," Van said with a grin.

"I mean, it's in his will. If the will is being contested..." I didn't need to finish that sentence by the way

Van's eyebrow quirked upward; I knew he understood the meaning.

"What do you think is the home's value, monetarily," Van clarified. "Not emotionally."

"I know my grandparents bought it for half a million. The last time it was discussed, Mom said it was worth over ten million."

Van shook his head. "In today's market it's even more. Granted, these old homes are now competing for the market with some of the newer luxury residences in the towers such as Vista Tower and 1000M. Nevertheless, they're still sought after."

"How do you know so much about Chicago real estate?"

"I buy and sell. Real estate is a commodity." He lifted his chin as the sedan creeped closer. "Besides the structure, there is a fair amount of land on this lot. Being in Lincoln Park, I don't doubt it would get an impressive price tag."

My lips curled. "You said you wouldn't be impressed."

"I evaluate everything for its worth. I admit that your parents' home is valuable real estate. I'm still more impressed with their daughter than their holdings."

"The will…" I began as the sedan came to a stop, my father standing on the sidewalk, personally greeting each guest and looking handsome in his tuxedo.

"We'll talk about it later," Van said as we scooted from the back seat into the chilled air. We'd chosen to not wear topcoats. My long cape sleeves blew in the wintery breeze.

Dad's smile broadened as he stared down at me. "Little girl."

Releasing Van's hand, I leaned into my father. Dad's arms surrounded me. Perhaps it was an act, but in this familiar setting, he appeared more relaxed than he had a few days ago at the board meeting.

Releasing me, he kept ahold of my hand and scanned from my hair to the pointed toes of the Jimmy Choo shoes. "Look at you," he said with a smile. "You're stunning." His attention then went to my hand that he was holding, the one that now wore my engagement ring.

Dad's chest inflated and deflated before his eyes met mine. "It's beautiful. Congratulations, to both of you."

"Thank you, Dad."

Next Dad extended his hand toward Van. "Mr. Sherman, welcome and thank you for convincing our daughter to attend this gathering."

Van shook his hand. "Call me Van, please." He winked my direction. "I had to acquiesce to her demands. Your daughter is quite the negotiator."

Warmth filled my cheeks.

Thankfully, Dad didn't ask for more details on the negotiation. I wasn't fully certain of the stipulations we'd agreed to. If memory served me well, it was something about making it up to me and being freshly fucked. Neither were conversations I wanted to share with my father.

Dad tilted his head toward the house. "Go inside. It's cold out here." As I started to walk, he again seized my hand. His voice was a whisper. "You should know, the board of directors and families are invited."

"Families?" Van asked.

Dad nodded. "Skylar is here."

"And other wedding guests," I said, my stomach twisting.

Van placed his hand in the small of my back. "Come, Ms. McGrath. It's time for your grand entrance."

"Everyone will look at me as the woman who left Skylar Butler at the altar and had the gall to show up to a party on the day of the canceled wedding with a new fiancé."

"No," Van's baritone timbre declared. "They'll see you for the strong and independent woman who kicked a weaselly cheat to the curb."

"And landed a better fiancé?"

Van laughed. "You did, but that's because of the strong beauty you are."

Taking a deep breath, I let Van lead me toward the opulent glass doors. It was difficult to believe I'd been in this house two weeks earlier. If I were testifying under oath, I don't think that I could articulate the immenseness of the changes in my life over that short period of time.

Not being able to give them words was different

than not recognizing them. As the doors opened, I felt the change within me. For once, I didn't have the sense of the little girl who grew up within these walls. The field was the same, but from deep within my soul, I knew I was different.

Smiling at the man at my side, I also knew he was the catalyst for that change.

My parents' butler, Arnold, greeted each guest at the door. "Ms. McGrath," he said with a nod as we stepped through the threshold. "Welcome home. It's very good to see you."

"Thank you, Arnold." I tilted my head to my side. "Arnold, this is my fiancé, Donovan Sherman."

Van offered him his hand.

For a split second, Arnold hesitated before offering his hand in return.

As they shook, Van said, "Very nice to meet you, Arnold."

A genuine smile came to the older man's face. "And you also, Mr. Sherman. Welcome."

Two stories above, a glistening chandelier sent prisms of light to the marble floor below, mixing with the reflections of the lights from the tall and slender Christmas tree. All the guests for as far as the eye could see were dressed for the occasion, long and short dresses in festive colors and men in suits and tuxedos.

Holiday music flowed through the air from the conservatory on the right.

I knew from experience that the music wasn't piped

through an invisible sound system. That wouldn't do for my mother. If this was similar to years past, I suspected that the grand piano was currently being played in conjunction with the rest of a quartet, historically, consisting of a string bass or cello, a violin, and a harp.

Forcing smiles and nods, I acknowledged the stares and greetings coming my way.

"You made Arnold's night," I whispered.

By Van's smirk, I was most certain he knew what I meant. No other guest would offer their hand in greeting to the help. It was the way it was, without question. Then again, Van didn't employ help, not in the traditional sense of the word, even calling himself a minimalist in that category.

If he were a minimalist, my mother was the opposite —pretentious.

Van's deep tenor cut through the background noise. "I save my smugness for negotiations and boardrooms. How long has Arnold worked for your family?"

"Since I was young."

"And in pigtails?"

I grinned. "Yes."

"And has he done his job?"

"Exceedingly well."

"Then by all means, the man has earned a simple handshake."

Our conversation stopped as a young man in a tuxedo approached with a tray of crystal flutes filled with champagne. I didn't recognize him, which meant that he was one of the catering team. It also meant that he didn't know me any more than he knew any other guest.

After taking our drinks, I led Van toward the back terrace. Despite the winter weather, there would be a large canopy with sides and dozens of tall propane heaters to give the illusion of warmth. It was also the location of the queen of the manor.

I continued my smiles and nods and saying hellos as we worked our way through the crowd.

Van leaned closer, his whisper near my ear. "You introduced me to Arnold, but not to any other guests."

"I care more about Arnold. These people are staring at me and thinking about how instead of here, we should be at my wedding. Whether they know about Skylar or not, seeing me here with you, they're jumping to their own conclusions."

"Their opinions are irrelevant."

I wished I could agree.

We paused as the hallway gave way to the expanse of the rear living room. A large perfectly shaped Christmas tree decorated with colorful lights and large ornaments was near the far end next to the fireplace. The usual pictures that donned the mantel were missing, replaced by more holiday décor.

This room was wider than it was deep, spanning the width of the house with multiple couches and groupings of chairs. There were also three sets of tall double-arched glass doors that led out onto the terrace. As if it were summer instead of the final day of the year, all the doors were opened.

I'd been right about the canopy.

Inside, the white tent was filled with round tables covered in linen tablecloths with tall centerpieces consisting of vases of twigs decorated with tiny white, silver, and gold lights. Some guests were already seated outside while others stood or sat inside. If we went to the left inside and turned left again, we'd be in my father's barroom. I supposed some would call it his man cave; however, there wasn't one piece of the décor that wasn't approved by my mother.

With cherry wainscoting, intricate lighting, and an actual antique bar that was salvaged from a tavern in Indiana, even I believed the room was impressive.

"My mother is out here," I said, heading toward the terrace.

Van's response was too low to be heard beyond our bubble. "Joy."

"Julia."

"Julia."

My name came from different directions.

"Saying hello to my mother is the obligatory greeting. After it's done, I want to introduce you to one of my best friends."

"Vicki?"

I turned to Van. "How do you remember that? I think I've only mentioned her once or twice."

He lifted my hand to his lips, brushing his warmth

over my knuckles. "Who is important to you is important to me."

The drone of talking grew louder as we approached the far-right end of the tent. Standing amongst a crowd of finely dressed women and men was Anastasia McGrath. To some it might seem odd for this party to go on with the canceled wedding and the questionable state of Wade Pharmaceutical. If I knew my mother, it was exactly why it had progressed. She wouldn't hide from her daughter's failed engagement or publicized problems with Wade. After all, she'd held court in this house since she wore pigtails.

For only a second, I recalled Grandfather's will.

If it is contested, could she lose the house as well as us losing Wade?

As Donovan and I approached, the sea of people surrounding her parted.

Mom's blue eyes met mine as she stood, her perfect smile in place. "Julia." She lifted her hands. "I'm so happy you made it."

Chapter 22

Van

"Mr. Sherman," Mrs. McGrath said, luring me closer.

Julia's mother's eyes widened at the sight of the diamond on Julia's finger. Her gaze went from the ring to me and back to Julia. As she inhaled, I imagined her response may be different if we weren't surrounded. Seeing as how the crowd around her was enthralled by her every word, whatever she was about to say was for them, not truly for Julia and me.

She clasped her hands as her best wishes sprang from her lips. "Congratulations."

"Thanks, Mom," Julia said, reaching for my hand.

I held tight knowing that while Julia was competent, sometimes the additional support of another person was the small bit of encouragement that was needed. In the short time of our relationship, I sensed that the only time Julia's confidence waned was in the presence of her mother.

"Mrs. McGrath," I said with a smile and a nod.

"Ana, please." She glanced at Julia's hand as her

cheeks rose in a polite smile. "It appears to be official. We are to be family."

"It's official," I said.

The crowd around us grew silent as their collective gaze stayed fixed on our trio.

It was Ana who made the announcement. "What better time to announce to all of you, our dearest friends...our darling girl is once again engaged. May I introduce her fiancé, Donovan Sherman."

Speaking up and commenting that Julia was not a girl but a woman was on the tip of my tongue; however, Ana had unleashed the masses. After a stifled gasp, all the women descended, hugging Julia and wishing her well. Simultaneously, a line of men formed, anxious to shake my hand and offer congratulations.

It was one thing to want to be a better man for Julia. It was another to give up my survival skills. The wolf was a predator always listening and always watching.

There was prey within my sights. I sensed their unease.

Unlike Marlin's interest for our private meeting the other day, he and Gwen were currently silent, no well wishes or even acknowledgments. I met Marlin's stare with a smirk and a nod. Before this night was over, I planned to plant more seeds for the sale of his shares.

This wasn't the time.

As we began to walk away, Ana called to Julia. "When it's time to eat, I have you and Mr. Sherman seated at our table."

Julia stiffened under my touch.

Without a word from me, her spine straightened. "That's very kind, Mother. I promised Vicki we would catch up."

Ana feigned a smile as she looked at her friends. "Well, it seems we have more room at our table. Who would like…"?

I led Julia away. Leaning down, I whispered, "I'm proud of you."

She nodded but remained quiet. Quickly, she replaced her empty flute with a full one, and we continued walking until we were away from the crowds in a more isolated spot.

Spinning toward me, her eyes sparkled. "That felt good. I've never done that before."

"I'm proud of you."

She inhaled, her pert breasts pushing against the red fabric as her matching lips curled into a smile. "I can really do this."

"Stand up for yourself," I said. "Not only are you capable, but you're also damn good." Looking beyond the competent woman near me, I realized that Julia had led us to the formal dining room. A chandelier hung from the center of the room. A lighted glass cupboard filled one full wall, and the table was set to seat sixteen. I scoffed. "It appears that you had nice intimate family meals as a child."

Julia took another drink of champagne. "We rarely ate in here. I think my mom did when she was young, but for the most part, we ate in the kitchen." Her blue eyes met mine. "Would you like a tour?"

"No."

There was nothing I wouldn't do to forever see the smile that broke out, consuming her beautiful face. "You're not impressed," she finally said.

"It's stuff, Julia. I get the quest for more. I have that quest. I don't acquire money or power to put it on display. I've found that those who do use it as a shield. They hide behind their spoils in order to keep their inadequacies from being seen. Just look around. Who would think that your family business had just narrowly escaped the brink of collapse? This home is their shield. Or maybe only your mother's. She does enjoy her status —the perception of her status," I corrected.

"I tried not to think about having money as a child. I didn't really understand what it meant. When you're young, you assume everyone lives the way you live."

"They don't." I reinforced the lock in my mind, the one keeping any lingering memories of my childhood at bay.

Julia's blue gaze flittered around the room. "The only time the differences became obvious was when I'd bring a new friend home. I hated it really. I hated when people would treat me differently after coming here."

"What about your friend Vicki?" I asked.

"No, that's part of what I love about her. We have always been similar. Her mother is a surgeon. Other than she wasn't home much, she was always kind to me.

Her dad's in banking." Julia's smile grew. "They got along with my parents but didn't fawn over them like some other people would. And my mother doesn't fawn over anyone. The mutual respect helped Vicki's and my friendship."

I knew the feeling of not wanting to bring people to your house. It seemed that as different as our childhoods had been, we shared some aspects. My reasons were different, but still present. "There is one room I'd like to see."

Julia finished her second glass of champagne. "Where?"

"Your bedroom."

Pink climbed from the neckline of the red dress upward. "Van, we can't..."

"Oh, we could." I lowered my voice. "Fucking doesn't get much fresher than that."

She shook her head, the small curls near her face swaying.

"I'm teasing you, beautiful."

Her blue eyes opened wide. "Mr. Sherman teases and cuddles. Wait until I notify the press."

"Definitely redact-able information." Before she could reply, I added, "I simply would like to see it. Show me a peek at the girl with pigtails."

"I'm scared."

I ran my thumb over her cheek. "You're too strong to be scared."

"I don't want you to think less of me."

"Because of your childhood room?"

"Because of all of this. I don't want you to see me as a spoiled child."

I leaned closer, tilting my forehead to hers. "I don't see you as a child. Seeing your childhood home and room isn't changing my opinion of the amazing woman I found in the snow. I've watched you go in and out of an outhouse and survive in a blizzard without electricity. Our childhood doesn't define us. Mine sure as hell didn't."

Before she could respond, her name was called from across the room, "Julia."

Both of our necks straightened at the voice that was unfortunately becoming too familiar. We turned as Skylar entered the dining room, on his arm a brunette wearing a long gold dress. I couldn't say if she were pretty or not. I could instantly sense that she wanted to be anyplace other than in this dining room.

"Mr. Butler," I said, filling the deafening silence. "It is nice of you to seek us out."

Chapter 23

Van

Skylar Butler turned to the woman at his side and back to us. "Mr. Sherman, may I introduce my date for the evening, Elizabeth Sanders."

Elizabeth.

Beth.

I nodded with a smile. "It's a pleasure. I've heard about you."

Nodding quickly, she released Butler's arm and came closer to Julia. "I asked Skylar to bring me here, hoping you'd be here."

"Beth, we have nothing to say to one another."

Beth swallowed as she rubbed her lips together. "I want you to know that I'm sorry. I didn't mean..."

Every instinct told me to seize Julia's hand and save her from this moment. As those thoughts went through my head, an observation caught my attention. It was Julia. While Skylar Butler was a mealy measly wannabe and Beth was a bundle of nerves, my woman was confident, radiant, and calm.

The calm in the storm.

She reached out, placing her left hand on Beth's arm. Perhaps it was because her right hand was holding her glass of champagne or maybe beneath her gorgeous smile, my woman was also a quick thinker and a bit devious. Nevertheless, with her fingers on Beth's arm, Julia's engagement ring shone like a beacon in the storm.

Beth wasn't the only one to notice the new ring. Though neither she nor Butler verbally commented, their expressions gave away their surprise.

It was Julia who spoke. "Don't apologize, Beth. I have no ill will toward you." She smiled up at me. "Without your announcement, I would never have driven to Ashland, never have met Van. I would have never known that feeling when two people unite, the flutter in your stomach that accompanies unchartable, intense chemistry. Believe me when I say I'm grateful. Without your announcement, I would have lived my entire life without that." When Beth didn't respond, Julia added, "I'm content. I won't accept your apology because I owe you gratitude."

"Julia," Butler said, standing taller. "I was wrong about what I said about Beth." He nodded toward her. "I was shocked. The baby is mine, there's no question, and Beth and I are going to have it."

Julia's smile softened. "I'm sure you'll be immensely happy."

"We need to talk about our house."

The house they were building together.

"I'll have our attorneys contact you for more information," I interjected. "Julia deserves her share." With that, I splayed my fingers behind Julia's back. "If you two will excuse us, I believe Julia was telling me about something she wanted me to see."

Her blue gaze came to mine. "Is there anything you haven't seen?"

Fuck.

Okay. That did it.

I was taking Julia to her room and fucking her for what she was doing to me. Her strength, wit, and comebacks were making me hard. Butler's expression, from the corner of my eye, was priceless.

I offered Julia my arm. "Shall we."

"We definitely shall."

"Have a nice life," I said as we left Butler and Beth in the dining room.

Instead of heading out to the crowd, Julia led me into the kitchen where the noise level tripled. A team of cooks and servers scrambled about. Motioning for me to wait, Julia went into the kitchen work area. As she floated amongst the chaos, she was a stunning red light shining in the sea of white and black uniforms. I watched as she went to an older woman, hugging, and then talking. When she returned, her smile was intact.

"That was Rosemary. She's basically the house manager. Everyone listens to her. I asked her to make sure you and I were seated with Vicki." She reached for my hand. "Come this way."

Turning a corner, she led me up a back staircase.

Once we were halfway up, I whispered. "I feel like I'm sneaking into your bedroom."

"You are."

My gaze narrowed. "Did you ever sneak boys up to your room?"

"Do you really want to know?"

"Fuck no. Besides, if it was the twit downstairs, I know what you didn't do."

The sounds from the first floor faded as we entered the second-floor hallway.

"How many bedrooms?" I asked.

"Six. Rosemary is Arnold's wife. They've lived on-site for as long as I can remember. When I was very young, my nanny also lived here, and I had a playroom-slash-classroom in another. Now it's just Arnold and Rosemary in one, my parents in the master suite, and my room. That leaves three bedrooms that sit empty in anticipation of guests who never arrive."

"I'm familiar with empty rooms."

We came to a heavy door.

Julia turned the knob and pushed it inward. Unlike the suites in my home, this was one large room with an attached bathroom. No sitting area or extra space. Then again, this home was built before those amenities were even considered. I stepped inside.

One wall contained a fireplace surrounded by built-in bookcases. The shelves were filled with books, pictures, and knick-knacks. I walked over and lifted a picture of three girls lying on their stomachs, looking at the camera, and laughing. I pointed to the girl in the middle. "You."

Julia was at my side. "Yes."

"I'd know your beautiful eyes anywhere."

She reached for the picture and sighed. "That's me with Beth and Vicki."

"Someday, you can all be friends again."

"I don't know."

I turned, taking in the large windows with thick sills and heavy curtains that filled another wall. Her bed was a canopy and smaller than a king. I grinned as I ran my hand up and down one of the four bedposts. "Can you guess what I'm thinking?"

Her cheeks rose. "Now you have me imagining that red tie and" —her breasts heaved as she turned toward the bed— "and the posts..."

In a few strides, I was across the room to where Julia stood. Tipping her chin back with my thumb and finger, I brought her lips to mine. "You have a very vivid imagination. I'm getting hard."

"We make a good pair."

"We do."

"We do," she repeated with a grin. "You're getting hard and I'm getting wet."

My lips met hers.

In another life, at another time, I'd fuck her right here, right now.

I had.

Not Julia, but someone else.

I'd done it to mark her as mine. I then watched as guests whispered at the wrinkled dress and messed hair. I'd done it because I could, and in hindsight, I realized that I'd allowed my *could* to outweigh the repercussions.

It was a conquest and nothing more.

The difference between then and now had nothing to do with how much I wanted to fuck Julia at this moment. The difference was that Julia wasn't a conquest to flaunt and even more importantly, she deserved better.

I could, but I wouldn't.

Julia was mine. That fact didn't need to be displayed by any means other than the ring on her finger. I also wouldn't because with time I saw that those whispers and looks from years ago were demeaning toward the woman I fucked.

Yes, I'd made many mistakes.

The last thing I wanted to do was make them with Julia.

With Julia, I wanted the opposite of what I'd wanted in the past. I wanted her to shine because from my view, out of all the guests downstairs, she was the star, a red nova to be envied, not ridiculed.

When our kiss ended, I said, "Thank you for showing me your room."

"No fucking?" Her blue eyes swirled with desire.

"Once I get you back to the hotel, plan to ring in

the new year as you come and scream without the threat of interruption."

"I'm going to hold you to that." Taking a deep breath, she turned a complete circle. "Before we go back to Ashland, I should come back here and decide what to have shipped to your house."

"*Our* house," I reminded her as I walked to her bedside stand. "You were living here before you came to Wisconsin?"

"I was. I know it's lame to live with my parents. I missed my own apartment. I had one in college, but with the wedding and the house Skylar and I were building..." Julia gasped as I reached for the handle of the top drawer of her bedside stand. "Van, stop. What are you doing?"

Even in the red high heels, she was next to me in less than a second.

"Let's go downstairs," she said, tugging at my arm.

"Oh, I was curious what this drawer might contain." She stood in the way, stopping the drawer from opening. I lifted her chin. "You see, I've heard stories about an unfulfilled sex life, and I was curious if my sexy vixen took matters into her own hands."

"You know I did. I showed you."

"Did you have help?"

"Jeez." Julia's complexion paled as she sunk to the side of her bed and covered her face with her hands. "Yes, there's a vibrator in there."

Tugging her hands away, I crouched in front of her.

"I won't look if you promise to be sure it's in your things to be moved to Ashland."

"Oh my God. Why does that turn me on?"

"Because, Ms. McGrath, I found the most perfect woman in the world, and I plan on keeping her."

"I'll be sure to pack it." She stood. "If we don't get back downstairs, there'll be rumors."

I offered her my arm. "Instead of rumors, let's show them the real thing."

Julia didn't lead me to the back staircase. Following the hallway toward the landing, Julia led me to the grand staircase, the one overlooking the foyer. As we reached the top of the stairs, I stood tall, my gaze narrowing as the crowd below came into view. One man in particular stood out. He didn't see me, but I saw him.

Fucking prey.

Logan Butler.

"Fuck," I growled under my breath.

Chapter 24

Julia

A hushed whisper subdued the conversations from the first floor. My mother's announcement of our engagement had no doubt skirted from person to person much as the game of telephone from long ago. As with the game, I couldn't help wondering about the complete accuracy of what was being whispered.

The guests turned our direction as Van and I descended the staircase.

"I was wrong earlier, gorgeous. This is your grand entrance."

Basking in his gaze, I lifted my chin as together we took the first step.

With Van's hand on my lower back, all the concerns I'd entertained about attending this party melted away. I wasn't a little girl or even my dad's little girl. I also wasn't marrying to fulfill a clause of my grandfather's will or to secure the McGrath-Butler connection.

With each step, a sense of pride and love swelled within me. Van was right when he said that love didn't have a timetable. None of my past or his mattered; we were a couple. Whether these people saw me as a capable woman able to make her own life choices or as a fickle child was irrelevant.

What mattered was the way the man at my side saw me, the way his green stare bathed me with the heat of his roaring desire. What mattered was the way we connected, not in front of this audience but when we were alone in our cabin.

The memory of me against the hotel window came to mind as warmth filled my cheeks.

There were stark differences between then and now.

One, I wasn't naked, and two, Van wasn't making love to me, not in the conventional way. And yet his presence and possessive touch filled me with the sense that I was his and he was mine.

The similarity to the window was what he'd said that night...about people watching.

They couldn't see us that night. Tonight, every set of eyes was upon us.

In this moment, I wanted every person below to watch and see the undeniable connection that we shared. Van and I may have happened quickly, that wasn't deniable. Yet for any of the people who held us in judgment for that, I felt only pity.

Pity that they had never experienced what we experienced.

Pity that they didn't know red sin.

And pity that they'd lived their lives without it.

Once we reached the marble floor, offers of congratulations met us. People I barely knew introduced themselves to Van, shaking his hand, and welcoming him as a member of the McGrath family.

From what little public experience I had with Van, I knew that being in the spotlight wasn't his favorite thing. He preferred privacy to publicity, a quiet dinner at home to a grand presentation. And yet as I watched him, that dislike wasn't visible. Van was charming, charismatic, and friendly. His ease pulled others to him. At this second, he was the opposite of the man described in some of the articles and even to who he claimed himself to be.

Van was in command despite any aversion to this situation.

Finally, a familiar face pushed her way through the crowd.

After shrill squeals, Vicki and I wrapped each other in a hug.

"Bitch, introduce me," she whispered close to my ear.

I reached for her hand. "I will." Rolling my eyes, I said, "We seem to be stuck."

"Then let's get you unstuck."

"Let me use you as an excuse. I arranged for us to sit with you."

Vicki's hazel eyes sparkled. "Oh, I've got this." With my hand in hers, she turned toward the hallway leading to the back of the house. "Excuse us. Excuse us."

I was helplessly tugged forward with just enough time to catch Van's eye and encourage him to follow. By the time we made it out into the tent, Vicki and I were laughing. It wasn't until her laughing stopped that I realized Van had caught up to us.

Before I could introduce Vicki and Van, he grinned, offering his hand. "The famous Victoria, I presume."

She stood tall, using the skills she'd mastered through life, the skills to walk the walk of the refined—it was an act and I loved it. "Mr. Sherman. I hear you want to marry my best friend." She winked my way while standing erect, waiting for his answer.

"Why, yes," Van replied, "that is the plan."

"Has Julia explained that there is a rigorous application process that must be approved—" Her words stopped as I wiggled the fingers of my left hand in her face. "Well, I suppose we'll need to fast-track the application process."

I wrapped her shoulders in a hug. "I've missed you."

She smiled at Van and back to me. "No, you haven't. I wouldn't miss me either." She motioned between us and whispered, "We need to talk."

More of the guests had made their way to the tables as Van pulled out a chair for Vicki and then one for me. As Vicki sat, she said, "My name is Victoria. I prefer Vicki."

He showed her his handsome smile. "I prefer Van from friends." He winked. "Be sure to let me know if I pass the application process."

Vicki's grin was ear to ear.

"Would you ladies like anything from the bar? I believe I'll step inside and be back in a minute."

"There are servers..." I let my words fade away, realizing this was his way of giving Vicki and I a moment. "More champagne." I looked at Vicki.

"Two, thank you."

Before he walked away, Van lifted my hand and brushed his lips over my knuckles. "If anyone asks for this chair" —his lips quirked— "be sure to tell them that it's taken."

Other guests were taking their seats at the table when Vicki reached for her napkin and used it as a fan. Keeping her volume soft, she said, "Okay, damn, girl, I get it. Where did you find him again?"

"He found me."

Her eyes narrowed. "I thought you applied for a job."

I covered her hand with mine. "I have so much to tell you." Warmth crept from my chest to my neck. "And so much I can't."

"Oh, that's the best part." Vicki leaned back, her lips forming an "o." "You've finally joined the club."

I leaned close. "If you would have told me how great the club is, maybe I would have joined sooner."

Her nose wrinkled. "No. I don't think Skylar would have done as good of a job at inducting you."

"I'm sure he wouldn't."

"Did you know," Vicki asked, "he's here tonight with Beth?"

"I did and I'm glad. I've moved on; he can too. It was also good to hear that he's taking responsibility for the kid."

A waiter placed flutes of champagne by each plate.

Vicki reached for hers. "Cheers, now we'll have two."

I lifted mine. "I'm already on three...I think."

"Here's the scoop," Vicki said in a whisper, "when Skylar told his parents the truth, they suggested that it would be best to get rid of the evidence."

"He'd made a comment to the like."

"According to Beth, having his parents tell him to do it put him on the defensive, saying he was tired of them running his life...like it ever bothered him before."

I lifted my brows. "See, this is working out for everyone."

Vicki shook her head. "I don't know. Apparently, there's World War III breaking out in the Butler household. You'd never know it to see them here, but Beth says it's bad."

"Excuse me," a man's voice said.

A smile came to my lips at the sight of Skylar's uncle. "Uncle Logan," I replied.

"Can an old man give you a congratulatory hug?"

"Oh, you're not old." I pushed the chair back and stood. "You don't hate me like the rest of your family?"

"You know Uncle Logan. I'm the easygoing one." He spread his arms as I leaned forward.

It's difficult to describe the uncomfortable sensation I experienced, similar to needles prickling my skin, as we embraced. I quickly pulled myself away and feigned a grin. "It's nice to see you."

"Be sure to tell that lucky fiancé of yours that Uncle Logan said hello."

Um, okay. "I will."

He nodded as I sat. Gallantly pushing my chair for me, Uncle Logan wished Vicki and I well and disappeared into the crowd.

"Did you think that was weird?" I asked.

"Yes. Uncle?"

"Skylar's uncle."

She wrinkled her nose. "Were you that close to Skylar's uncle?"

I shrugged. "I mean he was always around at family things. I never gave him much thought. His hug felt…" A shiver ran through me. "I'm overthinking. It's probably my nerves. I wasn't thrilled about being here."

"You've got this thing, Jules. You look…" Her voice lowered. "If I didn't know better, I'd say you look stunningly satiated."

Freshly fucked.

"Hmm." I looked beside her, seeing an empty chair. "Steven?"

She shook her head. "Ancient history. Maybe I can find a sexy older guy, one who doesn't play video games twenty-four seven." She frowned. "No satiation for me that doesn't come from my vibrator."

Holy shit. The vibrator.

Even the thought of it being in Van's control made my nipples hard.

Vicki was still talking. "...I could have asked Lucas, but when I learned you'd be here, I didn't want to have to entertain someone. I wanted to see my friend while I could."

"I think Van's doing the same thing, letting us catch up."

"Oh," she said, her attention going across the tent toward the house. "He's talking to Mr. Butler, Skylar's dad."

My stomach twisted as I turned. Van was holding two glasses of champagne in one hand and a tumbler in the other. Though they appeared cordial, I had my doubts.

"Do they know each other?" Vicki asked.

I nodded. "From a long time ago. I don't know any of the details."

Her volume lowered. "What's it like with an older guy?"

I usually loved Vicki's directness. Giving her a shy grin, I replied, "I don't have anything to compare it to. On a scale from one to ten..." I brought the rim of the glass to my lips. "A million."

Chapter 25

Julia

"The food is here," Van called as he walked toward the door to the suite. His long legs were clad in blue jeans and his button-up shirt was untucked with the sleeves rolled up to nearly his elbows.

Leaning back against the dining room chair, my soft sweater fell from one shoulder, revealing the camisole I wore beneath. It was then that I realized Van had my full attention, enthralling me with the powerful yet graceful way he moved. Donovan Sherman was the personification of a man in control—a wolf, a predator. Effortlessly, he commanded a room, whether it was with hundreds of guests, as at my parents' party, or here, with only the two of us.

And at the same time there was a calmness about him.

Do others see the calm or only the wolf?

My gaze went to the computer monitors before me and back to him.

Without a doubt, watching him was a better view

than that of the monitors or the notes I had flagged in my notebook.

As my core twisted, I knew the reason I stared.

Plain and simple, I enjoyed the view.

Van's deep voice resonated through the suite as he spoke with the hotel's delivery person, followed by the echo of the door closing. As Van came my way, carrying sacks instead of pushing a cart, his gaze met mine as if he knew I'd been staring.

Instead of mentioning the obvious, he replied to my unspoken question, "I was getting tired of the hotel room-service menu."

"I miss Paula's meals." Tilting my head toward the kitchen, I offered, "I can cook. I'd need to shop."

Van placed the bags on the one clear spot on the long dining room table. "I'm ready to go home as soon as you are. I'd rather you spend your time collecting all the information you need rather than spending your time cooking. Once we're back in Ashland, you can astound me with your mad culinary skills."

I pushed the chair back and stood, curious as to the delicious aromas escaping the bags. "I never claimed culinary excellence. I can cook and keep us from starving."

He kissed the top of my head. "I'm not incapable. I've been known to survive on coffee and soup in the cabin. Time is the issue. It's a valuable commodity. I'd rather pay Mrs. Mayhand to make the meals than to spend my own time doing it."

"You do know that her name's Paula?"

"She calls me Mr. Sherman. I call her Mrs. Mayhand. It's a thing we have between us."

My eyes narrowed. "Is it a good thing?"

"Yes." Van's response came with a nod and a grin as he began unpacking our dinner.

"Is there more to that story?" I asked.

"When I first moved to Ashland, I didn't know anyone. I bought a house, one that was on the property I still own. I'd left here" —he pointed his chin toward the windows and the lights of Chicago— "tired of people and wanting more privacy."

"Is that the house where you now live?"

"No, I had that one demolished." A shadow in his eyes was soon replaced as his smile grew. "The location is now a Christmas tree farm."

A warm feeling came to me, remembering our hunt for the perfect tree. Lifting a container Van had placed on the table, I found a large Caesar salad. Prying the plastic lid from the edges of the bowl, I plucked a crouton from the mix and asked, "Did you move to Ashland alone?"

The container in Van's grasp was the source of the fantastic smells. As he opened it, I saw the soft, buttery breadsticks and the air became thick with the garlicky scent, causing my stomach to rumble.

He replied, "Technically, yes."

"What does that mean?"

"It means that I was officially unattached."

Eligible bachelor.

I wanted to ask about Madison. It was on the tip of my tongue, but as Van shared, I was afraid to slow his momentum.

"I wanted to renovate the house," he went on. "I made the fortuitous choice of contacting a local contractor, Bruce Mayhand."

I smiled. "Paula's husband."

Van nodded.

"Wait, you renovated a house and then demolished it?"

His firm lips quirked. "Bigger, better."

"That's right."

He removed the last domed container. Through the steam-covered plastic, I made out spaghetti covered in marinara and two giant meatballs. I lifted the lid.

"Oh, that looks delicious."

Van went into the kitchen and returned with two plates, silverware, and napkins. As we both dished portions onto our plates, Van continued his story, telling me how Paula's husband agreed to do the work Van wanted. Over time, Van mentioned to Mr. Mayhand his desire to purchase neighboring lots.

"Always more," I said with a grin.

"Always more."

We carried our plates and settings to the living room, setting them on the table between the sofa and fireplace.

Van didn't sit, first turning on the fire, and second,

going back for water bottles and wine glasses. I retrieved one of the wine bottles he'd had delivered, one that we began the night before.

Soon, I was sitting on one end of the sofa, comfortable in my leggings and loose shirt, my legs crisscrossed while listening to Van as the fire illuminated the living room.

We both ate as he continued telling me about his beginning in Ashland.

"The Mayhands owned one of the neighboring lots. While they didn't want to sell, they were having problems, financial problems, brought on by unexpected medical bills."

I knew from my research that this was at the same time the Sherman Brothers deal was reaching its crescendo.

Van shrugged. "I saw an opportunity to get what I wanted and made him an offer, too good to pass up. I told Bruce to find a new house or find land if he wanted to build. I offered to pay for their new land and home, as well as pay additionally for the land he would sell to me."

"That was generous."

"It was the first time I had money, real money." He scoffed. "In hindsight, it wasn't much, but from where I started and for a man in his mid-to-late-twenties, I thought I'd made it big. It could be said that I was impulsive, and as my grandparents would say, too big for my britches."

I stifled a laugh at Van using such an old saying. "Obviously, the Mayhands took the deal."

Van nodded. "And in the process, I met my first friends in the area. You've met Mrs. Mayhand. I suppose that she and Bruce were technically old enough to be my parents. Somewhere along the line, they assumed a similar role. I would have complained if they'd been more obtrusive, but they weren't. They were just there for me.

"I'd made them a lucrative deal, and yet it was as if they didn't want the extra money. Instead of being put off, they embraced me in a way. I think Mrs. Mayhand saw me for the lost and erratic soul I tried to hide. At first, she would bring me meals, two or three a week." He grinned. "Each week, she'd stop by the office in Ashland with this huge picnic basket."

"You weren't paying her?"

"She wouldn't accept it, saying I'd overpaid for their land."

I pictured the older woman doting over me those few Friday mornings. "She has a kind heart."

Flames from the fireplace danced in Van's eyes. "Just like you."

"That still doesn't explain not using her first name."

"The first time Bruce introduced us to one another, he referred to her as Mrs. Mayhand. I remember thinking it was formal and wondered if it was a dig that I was younger, and once I got the chip off my shoulder, I saw it for what it was."

His various self-deprecating remarks had my attention. It wasn't like Van was saying he was less; he was admitting that he had room for growth. "What was it?"

"It was Bruce's way of claiming her, not as in Paula was an object, but as in she was his." He shook his head. "The way they looked at one another... I'd never before seen that kind of devotion...sure as hell not growing up." He inhaled. "Anyway, being with the Mayhands was as if I had been transported into some fifties or sixties television show with a family that actually cared for one another. Margaret included."

My cheeks rose. "I wish I could know Paula's husband."

"When he was diagnosed, I promised him that his family would be taken care of. I've kept my word." He grinned. "I usually do."

"Usually—that's intriguing."

"No, it goes back to what I told you from the beginning. I'm not a good man. I've made deals and then changed course when a better option became available. When it gets to the bottom line, it's about more and better."

"Helping the Mayhands isn't about the bottom line?"

"No. Granted, they are the exception, not the rule."

I recalled the Sherman Brothers deal and the lawsuits. "You're doing all of this with the Mayhands at the exact same time you were fighting lawsuits and slander over the lost retirement funds from Sherman

Brothers." I shook my head. "This is an example of the dichotomy that is Donovan Sherman."

"No, Julia. I'm straightforward—more, bigger, better."

"No, you're not. While all that legal trouble was hovering over you and you were being persecuted by the press, you vowed to take care of a family, one you now employ."

Van leaned back in the corner of the sofa, one of his long legs bent with his sock-covered foot on the floor. The other leg was extended on the sofa, that foot near me. He'd placed the plate with his mostly eaten dinner on the large table between the sofa and fireplace and settled back with his glass of wine. "I would say that I call her Mrs. Mayhand out of respect for Bruce."

Taking another bite of breadstick, I wondered how long it would truly take to get to know the man with me. I was becoming well-versed on the physical man, the hard muscles and warm skin. I could close my eyes and see him standing nude above me or lain out on the bed. I could accurately imagine the way his expressions changed as he claimed what I'd willingly given and the way his hardened cock filled me.

It was the inside of Van that held more mysteries.

Each insight he offered was a gift, an understanding into a man who gave few people that opportunity. Knowing I was in the minority gave me a warm feeling as I basked in that light of his gift.

"How is your research coming?" he asked.

"I feel like I need more. I've decided to visit the executive offices tomorrow."

Van sat forward, concern furrowing his brow. "I have meetings until three. They're virtual; however, if I cancel them, it'll be a rescheduling nightmare."

I squeezed his toes through his sock and grinned. "I'm a big girl, Mr. Sherman."

"I'm aware."

"I'm capable of taking an Uber or taxi to the offices." Before Van could speak, I shook my head and corrected myself. "Michael, sorry...the driver. Now, I remember your decree." I lifted my right hand. "I solemnly swear I will use the driver."

"It's not a decree."

"I was also thinking of stopping by Vicki's if she's home. I'd like to see her one more time before we head north."

I watched as the tendons tightened in his neck as his jaw clenched. "Tell me, can Michael drop me off at the door and wait in the car or will he need to enter her apartment? How exactly do we handle bathroom breaks?"

Van's eyes closed as his nostrils flared.

When his eyes opened, the intensity within was consuming. "This isn't a joke, Julia."

Seeing his reaction, I realized that I might have taken it too far.

"Van, I get it. I was teasing, kind of. I'm not a fan of the whole bodyguard thing, but if you think it's important as long as we're here in Chicago, I have no reason to argue."

Van hadn't confided in me that he'd hired a security team until after my parents' party. I commented about seeing the same man off and on, feeling like he was watching me. It turned out that he was.

"If I could keep you in our home forever, miles from anyone, I would. I'd lavish upon you anything your heart desired. I'd lock the front gates, keep everyone away, and keep you safe."

"I'm not a porcelain doll that can break."

"Growing up as you did, didn't you have bodyguards?"

I shook my head, his question hitting an uncomfortable chord. "That's the misconception I didn't want you to have after seeing my parents' home. My childhood and adulthood have been pretty basic."

Van scoffed. "I love you, but I'm confident you don't have a clue what basic is."

Unexpected tears prickled the back of my eyes.

Without a word, I moved my plate to the table and stood. I was only partway to the windows when Van was there, reaching for my shoulder and turning me toward him.

"I'm sorry, that didn't come out..."

I stared up at his features, the protruding brow, mesmerizing green eyes, and high cheekbones. "I told you why I was afraid for you to see the house, and now you're using it against me."

His hands were now on my shoulders. "I'm not. You believe your childhood was average because it's what you know—it's all you know."

"I didn't say average. I said basic. I did what other people do. I went to school. I had friends. I did gymnastics and dance. I became a cheerleader. I was on the student council and debate team. I went to college. It's all basic."

Van nodded. "Okay. It was basic. You also had a house manager, a butler, and a nanny. That's privilege, something I want you to continue to have. I was simply asking why you never had personal security."

"I don't know, Van. Maybe I was never threatened. Maybe my parents didn't perceive threats." I moved from his reach, spinning as my palms slapped my thighs. "Or shit, maybe I did and I was too privileged to realize it."

Van's jaw clenched and his Adam's apple bobbed as his hand trailed down my arm until our hands united, fingers intertwining. With my hand in his, he led me back to the sofa. As I sat, he offered me my plate with the remains of my uneaten meal. "First, your parents' bottom line doesn't compare to mine. I'm not saying that to minimize what they have, what you have. I'm saying that with more money and more power comes more reasons for concern. I want you to listen when I say that I perceive a threat."

Julia

a threat.

My appetite disappeared not only with Van's words but the seriousness in his expression. "Van, I'll use Michael for the drives and" —I shook my head — "if you want one of those other men to follow me, at least now I know who they are, and they won't creep me out."

"I should have explained earlier. That's on me."

I set my plate back on the table as Van resumed his seat at the other end of the sofa, his wine glass in hand. "Tell me why I would be threatened."

"Me." When I remained quiet, he went on, "I've said it before. My involvement with you and with Wade Pharmaceutical has drawn attention. Right now, there's a well-funded SPAC trying to purchase Wade shares. I've had my people digging. My people are damn good, and we're still coming up blank on who exactly is involved in the SPAC. Just yesterday they acquired the shares recently purchased by Wolfe Acquisitions."

"I saw the memo," I said, thankful I was receiving

real-time information. "GreenSphere still has only five percent of shares, the same as Aphrodite Corporation. I don't know if we know who Aphrodite is either."

"Five percent seems inconsequential," Van said. "Why obtain them?"

"I don't know. So, you think GreenSphere consists of people who would threaten me?"

"I'm concerned that whoever has invested in Green-Sphere is keeping their connection hidden. There are other factors at play. I've been upfront with you about my feelings regarding the Butler family. While we're playing relatively nice concerning Wade, I'm working behind the scenes. My people have gotten information regarding a few of Marlin Butler's other investments. An anonymous tip was made last Friday morning to the SEC. From what I've been told, they've taken notice."

My eyes opened wide. "The Security and Exchange Commission. You turned in Marlin?"

"The tip was anonymous."

I took a deep breath. "If Marlin is involved in something illegal, won't that bring undue scrutiny on Wade?"

"I've looked through the information you have with one goal in mind, to find something illegal at Wade. It doesn't exist. There are some interesting and maybe questionable practices from a shareholder's point of view. Yet nothing illegal. If Marlin finds himself in the hot seat with the SEC, his best move is to sell."

"And you want to buy." It wasn't a question.

"I do." Van's eyebrows quirked. "Speaking of Butlers,

why didn't you tell me that Logan Butler spoke with you at the party?"

"Uncle Logan." I shook my head. "I didn't say anything because there was nothing to say other than he gave me an odd feeling." I reached for a water bottle and twisted the cap. "It's weird. I've known him my whole life but there was something about his comments the other night that gave me the creeps."

Van didn't speak.

"It was probably more me than him. I have this preconceived notion that all the Butlers hate me, and he was *too* nice. Does that make sense?"

"Logan Butler isn't nice. I'm sorry he had the chance to get to you. I wanted to give you and Vicki some time alone."

"And I appreciated that. That's why I'd like to see her again before we leave."

"I don't like you out of my sight." He inhaled. "I'm not keeping you hostage, Julia. I want you safe. I've made enemies and letting Logan close to you was already a fuck-up."

"Uncle Logan is Uncle Logan. Maybe he's turning into a creepy old man, but he's harmless."

Van's jaw tightened as muscles protruded on the sides of his handsome face. Before speaking, his nostrils flared and his chest expanded, putting strain on the tiny buttons. "He isn't harmless."

Before I could counter, Van went on, "I've mentioned that Logan Butler and I go way back, back to before my name was Sherman and even before Sherman and Madison Corporation. We didn't get along back then, and then life moved on. Finding you has rekindled our animosity."

"Did you talk to him on New Year's Eve?"

"No. I saw him when we came down from your bedroom. I spoke to Marlin." Van took another drink of his wine. "When it comes to Logan, Marlin has a justified big-brother complex. He is actually Logan's older brother; he's also bailed Logan out of shit too many times to count. I'm confident that Logan is the key to taking down Marlin."

I was thinking about Van's comment about Marlin helping Logan. "I don't have a sibling, but I'd assume that's what brothers and sisters do for one another."

Van shook his head.

It was then I recalled the picture of the little girl with brown hair, the one Van said was his niece, Brooklyn. "You don't have that kind of relationship with your brother." It wasn't really a question; however, since Van was in a sharing mood, I'd do my best to learn.

His tone deepened. "We don't."

"What about your sister?"

"Did I mention I had a sister?"

I tried to calm the storm within me that his tone evoked. "No, you haven't. On the first day I met Margaret, she asked if I was your sister. Later, she used the name Olivia. I put two and two together."

Van nodded.

"Can you tell me anything about her?"

For a lingering moment in time, his lips came together, unmoving until... "This is where I'm asking for time and space."

Shrugging my shoulder, I took a drink of the water, unsure why his siblings were such a dark road for Van. I saw it as simple demographic information, such as where did Van fall in the birth order.

Simple was obviously not the way Van saw it.

When I looked up, I was struck by the change in Van's expression. Staring toward the fire, his profile was hauntingly beautiful yet sad. I ran my hand up Van's shin, beneath his blue jeans. "Hey, you're going away."

He blinked my direction.

I decided to change the subject. "Did something happen today? You were in the back bedroom most of the day, and I didn't want to interrupt you."

Van shook his head as if coming out of the fog. "My normal business. I also followed up on the email chain you showed me."

"How? Did you talk to my mother?"

"No, I contacted the bank and asked to speak to the representative assigned to the Wade Pharmaceutical account."

The small hairs on my neck stood to attention. "Because you don't think I'm capable of getting answers?"

"You, my dear, are capable, but not legally able. As a significant shareholder, I'm qualified to ask questions.

You were right. The balloon payment was in the original loan agreement; however, it was scheduled to come due two years ago. Your mother convinced the bank to hold off for a two-year extension."

My newly consumed dinner churned in my stomach. "I've been going through the ledgers; although I asked for five years, that's not what I have. I doubt Wade would have been able to make the payment two years ago."

"They would've needed to take the hike in interest rate or apply for another loan from another institution."

"Would another institution give them the money?" I asked.

"More than likely. Especially if Wade divulged the promising information on the Alzheimer's treatment. The second institution would charge an even higher interest rate, but most new loans can be negotiated with interest-only payments for a set number of years.

"According to the bank official, the email chain you found was your mother asking for another extension. Two years ago, she offered their home as collateral."

My eyes sprang open. "That wasn't in the emails."

"The representative sent me a scan of the agreement. The bank accepted her offer."

"Did she offer something else this time?" I asked.

"She didn't. That was why this extension wasn't granted."

I tried to keep the information straight. "You're

saying that the balloon payment saved Wade *and* the house?" I asked, unsure what to think.

"It appears as if it did. Again, Wade could have taken the higher interest rate and continued payments. The only way they would lose everything would be to default."

I shook my head. "I still can't believe I worked at Wade for a whole year and was completely oblivious to all of this. I also don't understand how my wedding to Skylar would've helped."

Van moved his leg as he shifted, leaning forward and refilling his wine glass. Before settling again, he took the water bottle from my grasp and replaced it with my untouched glass of wine.

"Are you trying to get me inebriated, Mr. Sherman?"

His lips quirked upward. "Perhaps."

"If you think that will help you take advantage of me, you're wrong. When it comes to you, I'm quite fond of being taken advantage of. I don't need any more motivation than your shimmering gaze or the way you change your voice."

"I change my voice?"

He was doing it, the rumble reverberating within me. "Stop."

Van settled where he had been seated earlier. "I'm not giving you alcohol to take advantage of you. I'm giving you a drink to soften the blow."

"What blow?"

"I have a theory."

"I'm listening."

"Once the shares diverted to your name, you" —he shrugged— "and I suppose Butler, depending upon how your prenup was written..."

I shook my head.

"You didn't have one, did you?"

"No."

"My theory doesn't make sense, even to a man like me."

"A man like you...?"

"I've told you that I'm a wolf in business. I single out prey and consume it, using it in a way that will benefit me, and then I move on to the next victim. Prior to Wade, the only deal I've made based on anything except numbers was the Sherman Brothers acquisition. I wanted that. It worked for me, but it could have destroyed me before I ever truly got my footing in this world."

"What are you saying?"

"The numbers with Wade indicate that it was a poor business venture for me to seize shares and finance a payment. I've looked at the research information you shared with me. I'm not a scientist, but it appears as though there's a long road from where Wade is today in its research and applying for FDA approval and patenting a medication. And yet your mother used her home, her family home, as collateral with the knowledge that the balloon payment would be due in two years."

"Why would she risk it?"

"Back to the theory about your shares. Once the shares diverted to you and Skylar, the payment burden would also." He shrugged. "Technically, it would be the corporation that owed, but as majority shareholders, it would be up to you and your new husband to secure the funding."

My pulse kicked up a notch. "And if we didn't or didn't know how?"

"You'd have been thirty-nine percent owners in a failing company and more than likely willing to sell at a low price to whomever would make you an offer."

I let his answer sink in for a moment, spinning the stem of the wine glass between my fingers. "It would have been my decision, mine and Skylar's."

Van nodded.

Wade would have faltered and failed under me. Another thought came. I met Van's gaze. "Instead of combining the Butler shares with mine, Marlin would have sold them, freeing himself from the burden."

Van nodded.

"What about my parents' home?"

"Theoretically, they could go to the bank with proof that they were no longer direct shareholders and ask the bank to secure another form of collateral or simply let the interest rate go higher. That wasn't a guaranteed out."

Millions of bits and pieces of information were

flying through my head. "Does this have anything to do with the contesting of Grandfather's will?"

"You were the one who mentioned it when we arrived at their house. Your parents inherited the house. If somehow the will was deemed in question, everything from Wade to the house would go into probate. Throwing the house into probate would be an incentive for the bank to seek another form of collateral. The process would take time and the house would be tied up during it."

"The filing against the will..." I began as thoughts came to life. "It was after they knew I was with you."

Van nodded. "Perhaps a change in plans."

I shook my head. "I don't believe my mom would risk it all."

"I'm trying to figure out the end goal."

"It's always been for Wade to continue and to succeed as its own entity."

Van nodded toward my glass. "Drink up. I have another option."

I brought the rim to my lips, tasting the full-bodied wine with hints of black cherry, spice, and vanilla. "Give me your second option."

"The damage was deemed irreparable. Your parents and the Butlers were waiting to jump ship once they were no longer at the helm."

"In that theory, Skylar was as blind as me."

"I don't give him a lot of credit for his intelligence."

Despite the gravity of our conversation, I grinned.

"I will say he sounded the sincerest at your parents' home with Beth."

"I agree." My smile soon faded. "I have to talk to Mom. I've spoken with Dad, and he talks in circles. I've attributed it to the fact he hasn't yet come to terms with me wanting a more encompassing role or maybe it's that he hates admitting the mess that I'm inheriting."

"I would tell you that your best option is to sell, but the interest from GreenSphere has thickened the plot. I'll support you in a sale and sell my shares too. I'll also support you if you want to keep fighting. The newest developments make me think there's more to this mess than meets the eye."

"Mess?"

Van set his wine glass on the table and stalked toward me on his hands and knees across the couch until we were inches apart. "The most beautiful and intelligent mess I've ever had the pleasure to be in."

Chapter 27

Julia

I used my knuckles and rapped upon Mother's partially opened office door as I stepped inside. The interior of her office wasn't much different than my father's. Mom's had a feminine touch that was hard to pinpoint. She and Dad shared a common space where Janie and Mom's assistant, Kathy, worked.

As I appeared, my mother looked up from her desk, her surprised expression indicating she wasn't expecting this early-morning visit. It had been four days since her big party, and while I'd spent most of my waking hours going through the information from Wade Pharmaceutical, I had to admit that Van's knowledge and questions had broadened my curiosity.

Van emphasized that he had no proof. That was why he framed them as theories—a rational type of abstract thinking used to account for a situation. It was my goal to move on to solid conclusions.

At this moment, trying to make sense of Wade's

recent decline felt as though I were pushing round pegs into square holes.

That was why I was here, why I wanted to talk to Mother.

When it came to Wade, she and I had been less communicative than me and Dad. I admitted last night to Van—and to myself—that when it came to my mother, I was less self-assured. I knew she'd been supportive and still I had trouble in her presence maintaining the assertion that I was capable of being on equal ground in the running of Wade.

Admittedly, the last few weeks had strengthened my resolve.

Van had done that.

He'd shown me that I was more than a pawn—I was a capable adult. Now it was time to make good on that.

"Julia." Mom's eyes went to her computer and her calendar. "I'm sorry, did we have an appointment?"

I shut the door, made my way to the chair across from her desk, and sat on the edge. "I called Kathy. She said you had a free slot this morning. I was hoping we could discuss a few things."

"Oh, Julia. I wish you would have called. While this time wasn't booked, I had it that way because I'm swamped. With the holidays, the party, canceling your wedding, I have so much to catch up on. Maybe you could come back. I know, we can go to lunch. It's been forever since we went to Palm Court at the Drake and had tea." Her smile brightened. "You aren't planning on leaving town anytime soon, are you?" Before I could speak, she lifted the receiver to her telephone. "I'll have Kathy call for reservations."

"I don't want tea, Mom."

Her blue eyes narrowed as she returned the receiver to its cradle. "You don't have to order tea."

I took a deep breath. "I'm here because I've spent the last few days going over the information you and Dad authorized for me to receive. Did you realize that it only goes back twenty months?"

Mom stood, her chair gliding backward. Her navy-blue skirt, matching jacket, and cream blouse accentuated her fit figure. In her mid-fifties, she was still beautiful. I knew it came with hard work and a strict diet. My mom wasn't the cosmetic surgery type of pretty. No, she took her health and appearance seriously. One could say a lot of things about her, but when it came to her workout and caloric intake, she was disciplined.

As she stepped around the desk, her nude Louboutin pumps clipped on the faux wood floor. Making her way to the ornate sideboard near the side wall with a coffee maker, she asked, "Would you like a cup of coffee? You prefer cream, right?"

"Mom, please sit back down and tell me why my information is limited."

"I'm not sure what you want or need, Julia. This is highly unusual for us to allow that data to leave our secure servers."

"I want to understand how Wade got to where it is."

Mom turned toward me, leaning against the sideboard with a mug in her hands. "Dear, I'm so proud of you. I'll admit I was shocked when you left Chicago. I never imagined you'd cancel the wedding. But now, Julia, you've saved Wade. You do realize that, don't you?"

"Van saved Wade, not me. And I'm not sure if he saved it or merely gave it a rousing jolt of electricity, a defibrillator of sorts."

"No. It's because of you." She shook her head. "There's been so much stress. Having even a sixty-day reprieve is a miracle."

"Is it?"

Mom went back to her chair and sat, placing her mug on her desk.

The city of Chicago was on display behind her through a wall of floor-to-ceiling windows. Fog and clouds filled the January morning sky with shades of gray as lights blinked on the top of buildings and spires.

She spoke, "I authorized the information back twenty months. I don't see how, if your quest is to learn about the new research, you needed to go back further."

"My quest," I began, "is all-encompassing."

"And what do you want to know?"

I sat back a bit in the chair. "Are you offering to tell me, Mom?"

"I can try. Wade has many moving parts. No one person is an expert in all things. I work as the conduit between our research team and the executive personnel."

"You're saying when it comes to the research, of all the executives, you have the most and up to date data?"

"I'm not a scientist. I don't understand the way cholinesterase inhibitors work. I know they do. I also know that the recent development approved by the FDA reduces amyloid beta plaque in the brain."

Damn, she was trying to out-talk me, using verbiage she thought I wouldn't understand.

Fortunately, I'd spent days reading reports, writing notes, and trying to assimilate what it all meant. I only understood enough to scratch the surface, but I could go tit-for-tat if that was her game.

I sat straighter. "Wade's research isn't on either of those mechanisms for treatment. Our research is focused on the early detection of amyloid beta. The hypothesis for Wade's trials is based on the data indicating that the accumulation of Aβ in the brain begins much earlier than previously thought, possibly decades. The pharma-cological compound Wade is researching is focused on the early removal of the peptides and amino acids from the interstitial fluid before they begin to accumulate."

Mom sat back. "Yes, the competition's newly approved drug is designed for use after the diagnosis. Ours could potentially stop the accumulation before severe damage is done." She shook her head. "I'm sorry I've underestimated you." She pressed her lips together, inhaled, and sat forward, leaning her arms on her desk. "This was supposed to go to you. It's what Father wanted."

"This? Supposed to go...?"

"Wade Pharmaceutical. You see, our testing has hit a roadblock. When undiagnosed patients are treated and subsequently do not develop the symptoms of Alzheimer's, it's difficult to prove that they would have suffered the progressive disease without treatment. Our mice trials showed great promise. The number of affected mice that developed the Aβ plaque is significantly less in mice that were treated with our compound. We have the documentation. However, as you realize, our compound is preventative in nature, not restorative."

"What about putting more money into the drugs Wade already makes?"

"Most have gone to generic."

"Why not create the generic ourselves?"

"It may be too late."

I took a deep breath. "If it's too late and Wade is losing value, why are there two SPACs interested in holding shares?"

Mom's blue eyes widened. "I don't know anything about that. Your father and Marlin are responsible for that aspect of the company."

I stood and walked the width of Mom's office. "Do you want to sell Wade?"

"Of course not. Wanting is different from reality. It may be our only hope."

"Did Van's interest help or hurt your plans?"

"Well, dear, he helped. He gave us time. The thing is that sixty days won't be enough. I'm afraid that Wade should entertain the idea of a sale or merger."

"What about your house?"

"What about it?"

"You used it as collateral."

Mom sucked in a breath. "That wasn't in the information you were given."

"No, because I'd need to go back two years not twenty months to recover that information. Mom, did you agree to use your home because you thought it was Wade's only chance or because there's a problem with Grandfather's will, and if that problem became common knowledge, having the house and Wade intertwined might slow the process."

She sat taller. "I'm sure you're capable of learning these details; however, I have to wonder what role Mr.... Donovan" —she corrected— "played. What does a man with his wealth care about this little company?" She stood. "I've spent my life, Gregg his, my father his, and my grandfather, to make Wade more and bigger. And where has it gotten us? We're on the verge of losing everything."

More.

Bigger.

My eyes opened to the reality that envy was a

common river that ran deep. Even those people I believed to be satisfied weren't. Everyone strived for the next ring.

"Mom, I want Wade to succeed in its own right. We don't have to become a household name like Johnson and Johnson, Abbott, or even Roche. It's all right to be in competition with only ourself."

"You're content to settle for mediocrity?"

"No. I'm satisfied to achieve success. I'm okay to contribute to the betterment of our customers. I believe Wade still has a chance."

The shake of her head was barely visible, if not for the way her spray of bangs swayed.

"The executive board is useless," I said. "With four members there's always the potential of a deadlock. Wade needs restructuring from the inside out. The ledgers you allowed me to see show unequitable spending that could be thinned. We have departments, whole departments," I said a bit too loud, "that sit like rotting fruit on the vine. Call Dad and the Butlers. Ask them to listen to me. I don't want a vote. I'll lose. I'm not asking, I'm telling. As soon as Van and I marry, I'm going to clean house. If you're tired, retire."

"Julia. This is my father's company."

"My grandfather. And he left the shares to me."

Mom's lips came together.

I went on, "Maybe he saw what I've never tried to see."

"What exactly do you think that is?"

"That my goal isn't to make me and my friends wealthy but to make Wade Pharmaceutical successful."

"Hmm."

"Say what you're thinking, Mom."

She stood. "I'm thinking that it's easy for you to take such a pious stand when you're about to marry Donovan Sherman."

"Maybe it is. And maybe if I would've married Skylar, instead of coming to this conclusion, I'd be running scared at the prospect of losing everything. It occurs to me that if one day I have a daughter, I hope she isn't made to walk a road that will lead to her own destruction."

"It was hardly annihilation for you to marry Skylar. It would have made this easier. The dominos would have fallen." Mom let out a breath and her gaze met mine. "Come back when the stocks are yours. Until then, your father and I are in control."

I hated that Van was right.

My stomach twisted in knot after knot as I reached into my purse and removed a letter addressed to my parents. "I was hoping this wasn't the way it would go."

Mom looked at the envelope. "Tell me what it says."

"It's a letter from Van's legal team on behalf of me, his fiancée, promising legal action if anything happens to my thirty-nine percent. It's a warning, Mom. Don't sell them or purposely devalue them. Forget the meeting. The next time you see me, I will claim them and then the dominos will fall."

She stood. "What? You can't marry without me there, without your father."

"Bye for now." I turned and left her office.

I made it all the way to the elevator before the tears escaped, sliding down my cheeks. Through blurry vision, I texted Michael.

Chapter 28

Van
Nearly fifteen years ago

As I opened the door to her dressing room, Madison turned with a gasp. Her emerald gaze softened as she took me in, scanning from my cheap rented shoes to the rented tuxedo. It wasn't what I would choose to wear. It hadn't been my choice.

"You aren't supposed to see me."

"I see you." I waited for her response or a reaction to my voice. Relief came like a breath of fresh air as Madison smiled, the skirt of her wedding dress swooshing across the floor as she came closer.

When she stopped before me, I reached for one of the small golden curls dangling near her cheeks, watching as it sprang at my pull.

"The wedding is about to start," she said, placing her petite hands on my shoulders.

She was every fucking thing I remembered and more. A woman like Madison deserved so much better than what she was about to get. I'd come with the plan to talk her out of this marriage.

However, now with my hands around her waist and her in my grasp, my plan was forgotten, replaced with the sweet scent of her perfume, the glow of her smile, and the desire in her emerald stare.

I lowered my voice, its cadence rumbling from my throat. "I couldn't wait."

It wasn't a lie.

Her face tilted as she grinned. "It's only a few minutes."

My fingers splayed, bringing her closer. "I want everyone out there to know you're mine."

"I think they'll get the picture when we say our vows."

I peered down her neckline, at the shapely half globes visible. "I want you, Madison. I can't wait."

Rose filled her cheeks. "We agreed to wait. After..." Her head shook.

After her affair.

It wasn't an affair. She wasn't married or even committed. It had been more than that, more to me.

My finger landed on her painted pink lips. "We've waited."

She sighed against my touch.

"I have something for you." I reached into the pocket of the tuxedo and removed a velvet-covered box. "I want you to wear this during the ceremony."

Madison took a step back and opened the box. She stared at the solitary diamond suspended upon a platinum chain. Her head shook. "It's too much. How?"

"I called in some debts. You deserve this, Madison. One day we can replace the small diamond on your engagement ring. You deserve better."

She looked from the necklace to the ring on her left hand.

For a moment I was sure she'd realized her mistake. I waited to be called out, but then it happened. A single tear rolled down her cheek as she wrapped her arms around my shoulders. "Thank you. I really do love you."

My cock pushed against the rented tuxedo.

She stood back, her fingers dancing near the string of pearls. "These were my grandmother's."

"I'll carry them in my pocket. I want everyone to see this diamond. It shines like you do."

Madison nodded and unclasped the pearls.

Taking the old necklace, I shoved it in the jacket pocket. "Let me help you put my gift on."

Turning toward the full-length mirror, Madison nodded. With her hair styled, her slender neck was exposed. Gently, I placed the necklace, purposely skirting my touch over her warm flesh.

In the reflection, I watched as her breasts heaved with each heavy breath and her green eyes stayed fixed on the three-carat diamond. After securing the latch, I lowered my lips to her neck and kissed her soft skin. "I need to be inside you. I want you to walk down the aisle with my come inside you."

Did she know?

Slowly, her gaze met mine in the mirror. As my pulse

kicked up, she reached for the full skirt of the dress, and slowly began to pull it upward. With each inch my cock hardened. It was as she pulled it up over her ass that I saw the white lace lingerie, the garter belt, the clasps holding the thigh-high stockings, and no panties. "Fuck." The one word came out more as a growl.

"I want you too." She peeked over her shoulder. "Now you'll know what I'm wearing and not wearing as we say our vows."

I held tight to the gathering of material. "Hands on the mirror, Madison."

Her body shivered as she obeyed, leaning forward and parting her legs.

I slid one finger between her folds. "You're soaked. All dressed in white. You should have worn red, you dirty girl." Her breasts heaved against the bodice as I freed my cock. "Don't scream. We need to be as quiet as church mice. This is our secret." She nodded seconds before I pushed deep inside her.

Her pussy clenched around me, reminding me of all the times before when I'd had her. This wasn't *our* first time, and *we* hadn't waited. This time was meant to ruin her for what was to come. To remind her how good it felt to have my cock buried to the root in her tight, warm haven. Her orgasm came fast and hard. I watched her reflection as perspiration dotted her forehead, her eyes closed, and she bit her painted lip to stop from calling out.

If I had her anywhere else, I'd make this last. I'd pry

ten more orgasms from her body until she was too exhausted to walk down the aisle or simply walk. We weren't somewhere else.

A few more thrusts and I closed my eyes. I imagined this beauty on her knees, taking my cock like the champion dirty girl she was. Buried deep inside her, I filled her, pumping stream after stream of come until she overflowed.

As I pulled out, I whispered, "No cleaning yourself." I nipped at her neck. "I want my come on your thighs. I want you to think of only me as they slide one over the other with each step down the aisle."

Madison nodded.

It was as our eyes met in the full-length mirror that I knew she knew. She knew my deception. "Don't disappoint me, Madison."

Yes, it was a warning.

Still leaning on the mirror, her eyes closed as a single tear slid down her cheek.

I didn't say another word as I put my cock away, zipped the cheap slacks and slipped away, out the dressing room door, down the hallway toward the back of the venue. I'd kept my head down and passed only a few of the waiters and waitresses. The guests and members of the wedding party were already congregating the other direction.

"Lip. Phillip," a voice behind me called.

I shouldn't have turned. It was the voice that made me do it. The one member of my family I didn't hate or desire to ruin. She was also the only one who would know my identity without a doubt.

"Olivia," I said, coming to a stop and turning to face her.

My sister was dressed all in blue, not unlike the color of the jewelry box I'd given Madison. Olivia's hand came to her lips as her eyes, the same color as mine, opened wide. "Van, what are you doing here?"

I shook my head. "You look beautiful, Liv."

She came closer and quickly wrapped her arms around my torso before letting go. "Oh God. I've missed you, but if Phillip or Madison sees you..."

"I was just leaving."

She reached for my hand. "I wish it was different."

"You know what they say, don't cry over spilled milk."

"Van, it could be different."

"No, Liv. The damage is done." That was true, but I was willing to inflict more.

"Call me."

I nodded, knowing that I wouldn't, knowing that any connection with me put my sister in a difficult position. I wouldn't do that to her.

With that, I turned, exiting the venue and walking two city blocks to my car.

I couldn't park my car at the reception hall. It would stick out like the beauty it was. Running my hand over the roof of the Bentley, a smile curled my lips. "Fuck you, Phillip. I have it all and you have sloppy seconds."

Ripping the cheap tuxedo jacket from my shoulders, I threw it in the back seat along with the clip-on bow tie. Unbuttoning the top buttons on the white shirt, I inhaled the warm summer air.

Seconds later, I drove by the front of the venue, imagining that Madison was walking down the aisle with my come inside her and my diamond—six times the size of the one on her hand—around her neck.

Knowing it was me, would she still wear the necklace?

Would she try to clean herself to rid herself of me?

It didn't matter. Madison knew it was me, and if I knew her, she'd confess. My smile grew, imagining that little conversation to kick off their honeymoon.

"For better or worse, motherfuckers." I lifted my chin. "Have a nice life."

29

Van

Present day

I stared at the text message I'd just received.

I'm ready to go to Ashland.

I should be pleased.

I was.

Julia wanted to go back to our home. I wasn't forcing her; she wanted to be there. Then again, I had the gut-wrenching sensation that things didn't go as well as she'd hoped with her mother. I sent a text back.

Come to the hotel.

. . .

My current meeting was proceeding without my full attention. Oscar Fields and one of his associates were doing most of the talking for my side. The screen before me was divided into squares. In the top right corner, the CEO of a failing logistics company was extolling the company's attributes. He was going on and on as if my team and I couldn't read a fucking profit-and-loss sheet. The company had potential. Hell, it was a booming industry getting shit from here to there.

Yet this company was losing money.

Someone had been skimming.

Is it the CEO in the top right corner?

As I listened to him speak, I found that something nefarious was the only viable answer for the loss of revenue. After all, the trucks were running. The trailers were full. There were issues with supply chain shit, but everyone was dealing with that.

The cause was inside.

If I bought this company, I'd fire everyone from the top to the damn janitor and start over. At the moment, I wasn't in the mood to figure out why this company was losing millions when it should be in the black. I quickly typed out a message to Oscar Fields, telling him to settle this deal.

Make an offer, make it low.

No guarantee on retaining employees.

No promises of fulfilling early release bonuses.

I'll pay for the damn bones.

That's all I'd commit to doing.

This CEO would argue and counteroffer. That went without saying. Nevertheless, he'd take the deal. He'd sacrifice every damn employee to free himself from the albatross around his neck. I saw it in his beady little eyes in the little square.

If this meeting were in person, I'd see the perspiration on his brow. As it was, his shaking hands were visible whenever he brought them before the camera.

I turned off my camera, eliminating my square from the screen.

My phone vibrated.

I'm on my way. First, I'm stopping at my parents' and making a list for the movers.

The hairs on my arms stood as if ready for a lightning strike. I told myself to be calm. She was with Michael. He'd already texted me before she did, telling me that Julia had sent a message to pick her up.

Hoping to make Julia smile, I replied.

Don't forget the item in the bedside stand.

.   .   .

She sent back an eye-rolling emoji.

I couldn't help the place my mind went. I adored Julia's spunk and her confidence. That didn't mean I wouldn't like to punish her for rolling her eyes. I had images of her, satin around her wrists, as I used the vibrator she didn't want to show me. I'd bring her to the brink and back, keeping her orgasm out of reach.

Shaking my head, I decided that those thoughts would be my ruin if I didn't stay focused on business. I honestly couldn't recall a time I was so easily distracted. That was what Julia did to me.

Disconnecting from the meeting, I called Connie.

"Mr. Sherman."

"It seems I'll be back in Ashland." Today was Wednesday. "I'm planning today or tomorrow."

"That's good news."

"Keep my meetings virtual for tomorrow. I'll resume what I can in person by Friday."

"Sir, he called again—Phillip."

I stood quickly, sending the chair flying against the hotel wall. He was still off the radar. The private detective confirmed that Brooklyn was at Olivia's home but no sign of Phillip. "What the fuck does he want?"

"To talk to you. He said again that if you didn't contact him, he'd contact Ms. McGrath."

I hurriedly sent a text to the private detective.

. . .

I need the whereabouts on Phillip Thomas. Hire other people. I don't give a fuck. I want to know where he is now.

Connie spoke, "Sir, he's abrasive. I'm concerned if I hang up, he'll do something to retaliate. I could block his number."

I pinched the bridge of my nose. "Connie, I'm sorry you're dealing with this. I'm going to have a trace put on the office phone. Maybe the next time he calls, we can determine where he is."

"I understand, and that would help, but now he's calling on my personal cell phone."

"He's what?"

Fuck.

"Send me his number," I said.

"Yes, sir."

"I can't legally ask you to trace calls on your own phone..."

"If it would make this stop, I will gladly look into it. I'll contact one of Ashland's detectives."

"I have someone who can help," I said. "Give me a few minutes. I think he can even do it without physically accessing your phone."

Connie scoffed. "That's a little scary."

"It is. You're giving me permission, right?"

"I am." She cleared her throat. "Does your brother have a drinking problem or...I don't know...drugs? At times his speech seems slurred."

I didn't know if Phillip had a drinking problem. I'd washed my hands of him over a decade ago. And then a thought came to mind. If he had a substance-abuse problem, was it affecting Brooklyn?

How often is she pawned off to her aunt?

This fucking had to stop.

"I'm not sure of Phillip's medical or mental state, Connie. It sounds as though it's not good. First thing, we'll find him. Next, restraining order." Or a bullet between his eyes.

I killed businesses, not people.

That didn't mean I didn't have connections. Lennox Demetri's family wasn't the only crime family that also dabbled in high finance. Chicago's kingpin was best known for real estate. Getting involved with those men for anything other than legal business wasn't my style, but I could break my own rule.

Exceptions existed for a reason.

Half an hour later, I stood near the tall windows with a TracFone I'd purchased down the street at a liquor store. After entering my brother's cell number and gripping the cheap plastic tigher, I heard the ring. "Answer the phone, you fucker."

The call went to Phillip's voicemail.

Hanging up, I called back.

Same voicemail.

The third fucking time he answered.

"Hello, brother."

My teeth ached from the pressure. "You're losing it,

Lip. Stop harassing my secretary. Leave me the fuck alone."

"Like you've left me alone? Like how you've left Mom and Dad alone? Like you left Madison alone?"

"Water under the fucking bridge. What do you want?"

"Oh, that's a broad question. Are you granting wishes, brother?"

"What will make you crawl back under the rock you've been living under? What do you want?" I repeated.

"I want the life that was stolen. I want the wife that was lost. I want a fucking family." His volume rose with each statement.

"How is Brooklyn?" I asked.

"Stay the fuck away from her. If you get close to her, you're going to prison. Lock you up, throw away the key."

I feigned a laugh. "You're good at that, aren't you?"

"I saw the announcement."

No fuck.

"And you called my office and now my secretary's private number to congratulate me. Your message has been received. Your rock is waiting."

"I want to meet her."

"No fucking way in hell," I said, my voice steady—the calm, not the storm.

"Leaving you alone with your money was one thing,"

Lip said. "I pictured you drinking yourself to death in your loneliness."

I knew what he wanted me to say, he wanted to hear my loneliness was over. I wouldn't. That would only bait him. I didn't care how much he hated me. I hated him too. I wouldn't allow this conversation to go beyond the abstract subject of Julia.

"Oh, here's the thing, Lip. I've never been lonely. I have got my memories to keep me company. I have a closet full of artwork. I have everything that you wanted."

"You know what happens when you hit bottom?" he asked.

"No, that's your specialty."

"Absolutely nothing to stop me. Nothing," he said, his words a bit jumbled. "Keep fucking with people's lives and my list of allies gets longer."

"Listen to you. We're not twelve years old and dividing up teams for a game of tag. Grow the fuck up. You're forty-one years old. Man up for once."

"Go to hell."

"You aren't at the bottom, Lip. You still have Brooklyn," I reminded him.

"You don't know anything about her. A ten-year-old girl needs her mother." His voice became more erratic, loud then soft, and then loud.

It was my turn for my volume to rise. "Stay the fuck away from me and my fiancée. I swear to God, if you get close to us, I'll have you killed. Money can buy anything."

"Not the woman you want."

"I'm not buying the woman I want. I have her."

Phillip laughed. "Bullshit. I saw her picture. You found some child who looks like her."

He was wrong. Julia wasn't Madison.

He was still talking. "...make her into what you lost."

"I didn't lose. You did." I took a breath. "And you're still walking. Bottom is six feet under. Leave us alone and you won't make it that far, not now, not when Brooklyn is waiting for you to go to her."

"You don't know a damn thing about her, and you never will."

"We'll call it a deal. I'll keep my word with Brooklyn. You keep your word and stay the fuck away from me and my fiancée."

"No deal, brother."

The call ended as I was left listening to silence.

"Fuck." My scream echoed off the walls of the Terrace suite.

That son of a bitch had been envious of me since we were young. Fucking competing and losing. He couldn't take it then and he can't take it now.

I paced around the empty suite, wishing that Julia was at the dining room table. I imagined her hair piled high on her head. I saw her sweet smile and the way her blue eyes shimmered when she smiled. I remembered our conversation last night and how quick her mind connected the dots. Fuck, she was something else, so much more than Madison.

Madison never had the drive for more, not like her sister or me and sure as hell not like Julia. Julia's drive might not be for money, but I saw her desire for Wade. In the early morning or the middle of the night, she'd make her way to the table as ideas came to her.

Julia wasn't Madison.

Fuck, Lip.

I found the woman of my dreams at a time I could give her whatever she wanted. Julia wasn't a replacement; she was an original, sculpted and created just for me. That's how out of all the women in the world, she was placed along the one road in the one storm for me to find.

Finders keepers.

My next call was to the security company I'd hired here in Chicago. I wanted double the men on Julia. I didn't give a fuck what it cost. Unless she was with me, there were to be eyes on her every minute.

As the gray sky began to darken, I stood beyond the front doors of the Waldorf, cold air swirling around me as I waited for the sight of Michael's sedan. The longer Julia stayed at her parents' home, the more self-control it took for me not to get in a taxi or Uber and head over there myself.

Pushing my hands into the front pockets of my blue jeans, I barely noticed the temperature. With each passing black four-door sedan that delivered another

guest, my skin tightened. And then I saw the car, spot-
ting Michael through the windshield.

I didn't wait for him to get out as I hurried to the
back door.

"Van? Why are you out here?"

Her blue eyes staring up at me was a fucking vision.

The world was right again.

Chapter 30

Julia

I placed my hand in Van's, his long fingers wrapping around mine. During the ride, I'd been lost in my own thoughts, but now, seeing him, alarm bells sounded within me. There was a change in his expression that I couldn't read. "Is something wrong?"

He helped me from the car and wrapped me in his arms. On the sidewalk, for all the world to see, we stood, me against him, his embrace tightening as the muscles beneath his shirt relaxed. His words were muffled.

As he finally loosened his hold, I looked up. The air was white with our breath. Beyond the vapor, I saw the man I loved.

"I've been worried about you," he said.

Taking my hand in his, we entered the hotel. As we mingled through the other guests on the way to the elevator, I leaned against his arm, taking comfort in his strength. "It didn't go well with Mom."

"That's what I gathered from your text," Van said before we entered the elevator, standing with other guests.

I was fine with our conversation waiting. I'd cried on the way to my parents and again while there, packing my things.

It wasn't until we stepped into the security of our suite and Van helped me with my coat that I began to explain. "I'm not sure how or when it went south."

Again, he wrapped me in his arms, one hand against my lower back as with his other, he lifted my chin. "Did you need the letter?"

I nodded as best as I could. "I hate that you were right. I didn't think..." I wasn't sure what I thought. "I don't understand what's happening or why. My gut tells me that you were right with your theory: Mom and Dad are tired and passing the mantle to me was their way of abdicating the responsibility for Wade's failure. But that leaves so many questions—the house, Grandfather's will, the SPACs. I just don't know."

The darkening sky filled the windows as the lights of Chicago came to life, one by one around the city, as if instead of a cold January evening, this was summer, and fireflies were flashing their lights.

"I'm sorry I didn't get back sooner," I said. "I do want to get back to Ashland, but right now I'm exhausted."

Van shook his head. "There's no need to rush. We'll

leave tomorrow. I was waiting to hear from you before calling Andrew and Ruth. Do you want to talk more about what happened?"

Tears blurred my vision. "I don't know." Stepping away from his embrace, I walked to the dining room, to the long table cluttered with all the information I'd tried to decipher. "She tried to dismiss me." I spun back to Van. "She said we could go to tea. Mom didn't... doesn't think I am capable. So...tea." I closed my eyes as my nostrils flared. "The last year working at Wade was a charade. It was busy work that made me think I was doing something, but I wasn't."

"Not because you weren't capable."

Taking a deep breath, I took in the man watching me, leaning against the archway with his arms folded over his chest, his long legs extended and crossed at the ankles. "How can you, someone who has known me for less than a month, think that and my parents don't?"

Van's lips twitched into a grin. "I've only known you as more, Julia. That's what you are. I don't see you as they do because..." He lowered his arms and came closer. Running his fingers through my hair, he said, "I didn't know the girl with pigtails and the Disney princess obsession."

I inclined my face to his hand.

"I only know the beauty and the warrior. I only know the woman who's rocked my world. I'm serious, Julia, you've tilted the axis and disrupted the orbit.

There's no possible way for me to see you as anyone else, as someone capable of bringing a man like me to his knees."

I could get lost in the depths of his eyes. The golden flecks glistened like snowflakes under a streetlamp, swirling in the depths of green. "I tried to be that person today. I failed."

"I won't believe you failed."

Shaking my head, I walked toward the windows, not seeing what was before me. "At first, she placated with tea at the Drake and then coffee in her office." The words rolled out, one after another. The flow increased as if the dam I'd tried to hold since leaving Mom's office had burst.

And through each word, Van listened, truly listening to not only my sentences but my emotions. I continued recounting what happened from the appeasement, to the vocabulary regarding research that was meant to speak over me, all the way to the suggestion that my motivation hinged on being married to Van. As each word, phrase, and sentence came forth, my sadness morphed into disappointment and resolve.

"She said you'd be more willing to let Wade fail if you were married to Butler?" Van asked, repeating what I'd said.

Turning away from the windows, I looked at him and nodded. "She said my attitude is jaded because I'm marrying you."

"How did I jade your attitude?"

A smile curled my lips. "In many ways, Mr. Sherman. But she meant because of your wealth." I sighed. "I've given that a lot of thought while I packed my things, and I decided she's right and she's wrong. You see, me knowing that you can financially back Wade gives me a safety net I wouldn't otherwise have had."

"How is she wrong?"

I shook my head. "I don't want you to throw good money after bad. I won't ask you to spend another cent to support Wade."

Van came closer. "You don't need to ask. I'm a stockholder, and I want Wade to succeed. I believe it can." He ran his touch over my cheek. "I *know* it can because I know you, not the child but the incredible woman." He trailed his fingers down my cheek, my neck, to the top of my scooped neckline, stopping between my breasts. "And in here, beating beneath my touch is a pure heart. I know that because I know the opposite. I see your light and your desire. You want Wade to succeed. That makes me want the same thing."

"I'm so tired."

"We'll go back to Ashland tomorrow."

"I want to get married."

Van's smile grew. "Me too."

"That works well."

"Tomorrow before we go back?" he asked.

I shook my head. "I don't want a big wedding. I

walked away from one of those. Do you think you could find a judge or a pastor in Ashland?"

His eyes shimmered. "I know a few."

"I was thinking that we could invite Paula, Mrs. Mayhand," I corrected, "and Margaret and her husband. They're your friends and mine. I'd like Vicki to be there if it's possible."

"Julia, anything is possible."

"I was wondering if we marry in the cabin with a fire and serve our guests coffee and nectarines?"

Van leaned down, bringing his forehead to mine. "If Mrs. Mayhand is invited, I doubt she'll settle for coffee and nectarines."

"I'm not my mother." I blinked away the tears. "I'm not."

"No, beautiful, you are not."

"I don't care about grand productions or throwing parties she probably can't afford."

Van shook his head. "I love that about you."

"Do you know that since we've met, you've listened to me more than almost anyone. You know more about me because you—"

"Care," Van said, finishing my sentence. "I care, Julia."

I wrapped my arms around his torso. "I love you."

Kisses came to the top of my head. "I love you too. I have an idea. We need to get our things packed, but that can wait. How about I order dinner and you go down the hall and relax?"

Peering up, I said, "A bath sounds nice."

"Take a bath."

"Would you like to join me?"

I grinned. "The bathtub is big for just one person. What about dinner?"

"I'm not hungry."

Chapter 31

Van

The master bedroom bath contained a large rectangular tub with windows that looked out onto the balcony and beyond. As Julia ran the warm water, I dimmed the lights, certain that when it came to this lovely woman, I didn't want the world to watch. I wanted her all to myself.

My earlier concerns evaporated at the moment Julia's blue stare met mine and she stepped from the car in front of the hotel. It wasn't my style to show public displays of affection, but in that second, I didn't give a shit who saw. The thoughts and worries I'd battled all afternoon vanished with her in my arms.

Soon we'd be back to Ashland, in our snow globe, a place I could control. I'd already called Jonathon Curry, Margaret's husband, and asked him to contract a new and improved security company. The property was too large for a fence; however, the roads to and from each building could be monitored. The main gate could be improved. Other gates could be installed. Cameras could be added with motion detection. I'd probably get a thousand notifications for deer and foxes—the only mammals I wanted getting close.

Leaning against the vanity, I grinned as Julia began to undress. It wasn't a striptease as she'd done weeks ago at my request. No, her movements were slow, unbuttoning her blouse and unbuckling her belt. Her back was to me as she was lost in her thoughts. It was as the blouse and slacks hit the bathroom floor that she turned, her eyes wide, her lips parted as she caught me watching.

Finally, her smile formed. "Do you like what you see?"

"No," I replied, my voice dropping an octave.

In two steps I was close, lifting her chin as her blue gaze met mine. "I love what I see. Every inch of you is perfection." I tilted my head. "There is one thing..."

"What?"

I brought my palms to her temples. "Stop thinking about today."

Julia sighed. "I didn't tell you about packing."

"Tell me in the tub."

She nodded.

Soon, my clothes joined Julia's as she removed her bra and stepped out of her panties. Reclining in the hot water near the far end, I offered my hand as she stepped over the side and settled her tight ass between my legs with her back against my chest. Wrapping my arms around her, I exhaled. "I don't think I answered you before, but I love your plan."

"What plan?"

"Our wedding. I'm free tomorrow night."

Julia quaked as the air filled with her laugh. "Let's say a week from Saturday. That will give me time to plan with Paula and Margaret. And I didn't get to see Vicki, but I can call and ask her to come north.

"Maybe before we leave, I can go to one of the department stores and get a dress." She didn't wait for me to reply. "No. I remember Margaret saying there are nice boutiques in Ashland."

I cupped some water and rained it over her slender shoulders. "You do whatever you need to do to make our wedding exactly what you want. After all, it's a first for both of us."

Julia's gaze came over her shoulder. "I believe you."

"Now isn't the time to discuss her, but I want you to know that there's no competition. There was a time when I was obsessed with Madison. I'm in love with you."

Julia settled against my chest. "The only important detail for our wedding is the man who says his vows with me. I want him to be you."

"Deal, beautiful, you have me. Do you want to tell me about packing?"

She craned her neck backward and grinned. "I brought what you wanted."

My eyebrows arched. "As in you brought it with you or you packed it?"

"Brought. I didn't want Rosemary or anyone moving boxes to find it."

"I like the way you think."

Exhaling, her weight settled again against my chest. "Rosemary helped me. She has been around since I was young. When she came into my room, I was crying." Julia shook her head. "She understood and had boxes brought up. We packed everything I want."

It broke my fucking reawakened heart to hear her say that, and yet there was another reaction, one that I couldn't completely describe. Julia was opening up, sharing her pain. Experience told me that doing what she was doing was more difficult than sharing our bodies. While sex was an intimate act, baring one's soul was a thousand steps beyond that.

I continued to rain the warm water over her soft skin, her shoulders, her arms, and her legs as Julia continued to talk.

"I think after the meeting with my mom, the act of packing felt final—irrevocable."

"You were planning to move from their house anyway," I said.

"I was, but I imagined it to be more festive, a celebration." Her head shook. "This felt as though I was closing a door on everything I've known."

"That's not what's happening. Your parents will always be your parents."

"You walked away from yours."

She wasn't wrong. Julia's situation was different.

"You have a connection. Wade Pharmaceutical will always be your family's company. The only difference is that soon I will be a part of that too—part of your family. You aren't leaving forever. You've grown and blossomed. Your petals have opened. I see you that way. Once you take your rightful place at Wade, others will see you that way. How your parents see you is immaterial. There is only one person's vision of you that matters."

Peering over her shoulder, her eyes sparked. "And you love me."

"I do, but I wasn't talking about me. I was talking about you. Julia, the most important person is how you see yourself."

She nodded and pointed through the windows. "Look out there. Do you think we can be seen?"

"That's why I dimmed the lights. I want you to myself." I reached around, finding the place where I could give her some release. "Spread your legs and keep your head against me."

"Van."

"Shh. Let me help you."

I parted her folds, dipping my fingers into her warm haven. With my thumb running circles over her clit, I pushed inside her. Two fingers. Julia's grip of my arms tightened. Peppering her neck and shoulder with kisses, I continued moving in and out. A pinch of her clit and her hips bucked.

"Oh, Van."

"Hold on, beautiful. Cover my fingers with your come." In and out, the water moved the faster my hand went. My other hand went to her breasts, caressing and tweaking her nipples. All at once, Julia leaned forward, calling out my name as her pussy pulsated, bathing my fingers in her essence.

For a moment, she lay back against my chest as her breathing resumed a normal cadence.

After a bit, the water sloshed as Julia moved to her knees and turned. She was stunning. Salacia—the Roman divinity of the sea—paled in comparison. Julia's nipples were red and still beaded. Water dripped from her pinkened skin, rolling down her pert breasts.

"I've never made love in a bathtub."

A smile lifted my cheeks. "I seem to recall a few times in the shower."

"Never in a tub."

"You know how I feel about firsts," I said with a grin. Having her come in my grasp had my cock hard and ready to go. "Come here."

I moved forward as Julia moved closer, placing her knees on either side of my legs. Holding tightly to her hips, her perfect round tits were right in front of me. Leaning forward I seized one nipple and then the next, licking and sucking. As Julia's hands came to my shoulders, I lined the tip of my cock up with her core. Her knees flexed as I pulled her hips down, sheathing my cock in her tight, warm pussy.

My neck strained as I became lost in the sensation that was her.

Fuck, she felt amazing.

Up and down she moved, her lips parted as water spilled from the sloshing waves and the bathroom filled with her assortment of sounds. Words interspersed from her and from me and yet it was the undistinguishable noises that encouraged our motion, the magic friction of our union.

As her movements sped up, my balls tightened. The pressure was almost unbearable—a volcano about to erupt.

"Fuck," I called out as Julia's pussy constricted and her fingernails scratched my shoulders. I pulled her hips down, holding her to me as my cock throbbed within her trembling core. Finally, her forehead dropped to my shoulder and our hearts pounded against one another's.

When she lifted her head, Julia's expression of pure bliss was one I could gaze upon for eternity. Her lips curled and her blue orbs sparkled. "I think I'm hungry now."

Chapter 32

Julia

"It seems like we're leaving with more than we came with," I said with a giggle. "And that doesn't include all my things from the house."

"I sent one of the men we hired over there earlier this morning." Van shook his head. "Some of it will make the plane ride, but since you also wanted your car in Ashland, the rest will follow in a few days."

I waved my hand. "I don't care. I just want to get home."

We were both dressed for our flight, him in his jeans, boots, and a button-down shirt with a sports coat and me in soft gray slacks, boots, my camisole, and a long sweater.

Van pulled me to him, kissing my lips. "I love to hear you call Ashland home."

"Get used to it. Once we say our vows in the place we first became one, you're stuck with me forever."

"I want longer."

I grinned. "Always more."

"Always more. And your things, you're moving into my bedroom. No more separate suites."

"You can be bossy."

"No one has ever told me that before."

Before I could respond, a knock came from the suite door.

Van placed one more kiss on my lips. "Are you ready to go?"

I looked around at all the bags including my over-stuffed satchel with my laptop and all my notes. Pulling my coat from the chair, I said, "I'm ready."

He opened the door to a bellman and a cart. "Mr. Sherman."

"Yes, sir," Van replied. "Everything is here." He pointed to our packed bags.

I stood taller. "I'm not quitting on Wade, Van. I meant what I told Mom when I said I'd clean house. If that means her and Dad and the Butlers, then fuck it."

Van's lips curled into a smile. "I have no doubt that I've made a good investment."

"I can't promise you did. I can promise that I'll do my best, and my odds of success are higher because I have a great teacher."

Van reached for my hand. "Shall we go?"

"We shall."

As we reached the first floor and were on our way to the front desk, Van's phone rang.

His brow furrowed. "I should take this."

"I can wait."

"The car is here," he said, nodding to a man who I now knew was a bodyguard.

"Okay," I said. "Don't be long."

Walking through the lobby, I turned back, not seeing where Van had gone.

"Ms. McGrath," the bodyguard said.

"I'm coming." It was then I remembered that I'd separated my purse from my satchel and laid it on the chair with my coat. "Shoot. I think I left my purse in the room. Do you mind if I run back up there?"

The large man shook his head.

"I'm new to this bodyguard thing. What exactly is your job?"

"Right now, it's to watch you."

I smiled. "Then I guess you're coming with me. It won't take long."

In only a few minutes, the man and I made it to the suite, found my purse, and were back to the elevator. "I'm glad I remembered that."

"Yes, ma'am. I texted Mr. Sherman about our detour."

Apparently, his job was watching and tattling. I didn't care, finding it a bit over the top.

The elevator doors opened to a full lobby. Nowhere in the crowd did I see Van. "Maybe he's out to the car."

The black sedan was waiting as the man and I stepped outside. As we walked closer, the man opened the door and peered in. "Mr. Sherman, sorry for the delay." He held the door for me.

"Hi," I grinned. "I tried to leave my purse."

"Julia."

I turned to Van, feeling an unusual uneasiness. "Is something wrong? Does it have to do with your call?" As I asked the question, the car moved away from the curb and onto the street. It was then I noticed the driver's reflection in the rearview mirror. "What happened to Michael?"

Van laid his hand over mine. "I've decided to change our plans."

Chapter 33

Van

A few moments earlier

I watched as Julia walked away with one of the bodyguards, pausing to send me a sexy smile over her shoulder. It was a grin I could never tire of seeing. Eyeing the bodyguard, I nodded. I'd seen him around throughout the week. I could trust him—it's what I told myself as I answered the call.

Hitting the green button on the phone, I connected the private detective's call. "What do you have for me?"

"He's in Chicago."

"Phillip?"

"Yes, sir. He was slippery about it. Three days ago, his bank account received an interesting deposit. It didn't feel right. I started digging. The shell company is layered in shell companies. Today, the transaction came up."

"What transaction?" Hurry the fuck up was what I wanted to say.

"Airline ticket. Seems that your twin has been in Chicago since yesterday."

"He's not my twin; he's my triplet." Only Phillip and I are identical. Wrong word. We look alike. Olivia escaped that hell, coming out with blond hair. All three of us shared the same fucking green eyes as our bitch of a mother.

"Fuck," I mumbled. "Fuck him, we're leaving the city in the next hour." I looked over the crowd. Michael's car was out front, but I didn't see Julia. "Where in Chicago is he?"

"I found footage of him meeting with a man yesterday at a restaurant west of the city. I'll send you the picture from the security camera."

My phone pinged.

I tried to keep my voice low. It wasn't easy as the concoction of anxiety and rage was growing, a cauldron, bubbling to the surface. "Where in Chicago? I need a fucking pinpoint location."

"I-I'm working on it. I can't find hotel reservations under his name or any tied to his credit cards. That's why I didn't call sooner. I wanted to give you more. I'm sorry, Mr. Sherman, I thought you'd want to know that he's where you are."

I do.

Shit.

I ran my hand over my face. "Find him and keep him tailed until Ms. McGrath and I are out of the city."

"Yes, sir."

After hanging up, I saw a text message from an unknown number.

. . .

Ms. McGrath forgot her purse. I'm escorting her to the suite and back to the car.

I exhaled as I checked the attachment the private detective sent. "Fuck, it was a grainy picture of Phillip and Logan Butler." I would bet my company that Logan was the provider of Phillip's recent income, maybe the reservations were under his name. "What do you two have planned?"

Shaking my head, I sent my hypothesis to the private eye and made my way toward the front door.

"Mr. Sherman," the bodyguard said, his eyes wide as we passed in the rotating door.

I stepped out onto the sidewalk, and he soon followed. "Sir, how are you here?"

My heart thudded against my chest as I looked around. "Where is Ms. McGrath?"

"Sir, you were here. I saw you."

My circulation sped as I stepped forward, reaching for the man's collar. "Where is my fiancée?"

"She left."

"What the fuck did you say?"

"Mr. Sherman, she left with you."

* * *

Thank you for continuing Van and Julia's journey with *GREEN ENVY*.

You won't want to miss a moment of Van and Julia's story as Van's past threatens Julia's future. There are more twists and turns, and sexy times to come along as the Sin Series continues in book three, *GOLD LUST*.

If you enjoyed *GREEN ENVY*, you can also check out the recently completed DEVIL'S Series Duet, beginning with the free prequel "Fate's Demand" and book one *DEVIL'S DEAL* and Aleatha's dangerous mafia stand-alone romance *KINGDOM COME*.

Turn back to *Books by Aleatha* for a complete and up-to-date listing of all the stories Aleatha has to offer.

WHAT TO DO NOW

LEND IT: Did you enjoy *GREEN ENVY*? Do you have a friend who'd enjoy *GREEN ENVY*? *GREEN ENVY* may be lent one time. Sharing is caring!

RECOMMEND IT: Do you have multiple friends who'd enjoy my dark romance with twists and turns and an all new sexy and infuriating anti-hero? Tell them about it! Call, text, post, tweet...your recommendation is the nicest gift you can give to an author!

REVIEW IT: Tell the world. Please go to the retailer where you purchased this book, as well as Goodreads, and write a review. Please share your thoughts about *GREEN ENVY* on:

*Amazon, *GREEN ENVY* Customer Reviews

*Barnes & Noble, *GREEN ENVY,* Customer Reviews

*iBooks, *GREEN ENVY* Customer Reviews

* BookBub, *GREEN ENVY* Customer Reviews

*Goodreads.com/Aleatha Romig

Books by ALEATHA

SIN SERIES:

WHITE RIBBON

August 2021

RED SIN

October 2021

GREEN ENVY

January 2022

UNDERWORLD KINGS:

KINGDOM COME

Stand-alone romantic suspense

DEVIL'S SERIES (Duet):

Prequel: "FATES DEMAND"

Prequel - March 18

DEVIL'S DEAL

May 2021

ANGEL'S PROMISE

June 2021

WEB OF SIN:

SECRETS

October 2018

LIES

December 2018

PROMISES

January 2019

TANGLED WEB:

TWISTED

May 2019

OBSESSED

July 2019

BOUND

August 2019

WEB OF DESIRE:

SPARK

Jan. 14, 2020

FLAME

February 25, 2020

ASHES

April 7, 2020

DANGEROUS WEB:

Prequel: "Danger's First Kiss"

DUSK

November 2020

DARK

January 2021

DAWN

February 2021

* * *

THE INFIDELITY SERIES:

BETRAYAL

Book #1

October 2015

CUNNING

Book #2

January 2016

DECEPTION

Book #3

May 2016

ENTRAPMENT

Book #4

September 2016

FIDELITY

Book #5

January 2017

＊ ＊ ＊

THE CONSEQUENCES SERIES:

CONSEQUENCES

(Book #1)

August 2011

TRUTH

(Book #2)

October 2012

CONVICTED

(Book #3)

October 2013

REVEALED

(Book #4)

Previously titled: Behind His Eyes Convicted: The Missing Years

June 2014

BEYOND THE CONSEQUENCES

(Book #5)

January 2015

RIPPLES (Consequences stand-alone)

October 2017

CONSEQUENCES COMPANION READS:

BEHIND HIS EYES-CONSEQUENCES

January 2014

BEHIND HIS EYES-TRUTH

March 2014

* * *

STAND ALONE MAFIA THRILLER:

PRICE OF HONOR

Available Now

* * *

THE LIGHT DUET:

Published through Thomas and Mercer Amazon exclusive

INTO THE LIGHT

June 2016

AWAY FROM THE DARK

October 2016

* * *

TALES FROM THE DARK SIDE SERIES:

INSIDIOUS

(All books in this series are stand-alone erotic thrillers)

Released October 2014

* * *

ALEATHA'S LIGHTER ONES:

PLUS ONE

Stand-alone fun, sexy romance

May 2017

ANOTHER ONE

Stand-alone fun, sexy romance

May 2018

ONE NIGHT

Stand-alone, sexy contemporary romance

September 2017

A SECRET ONE

April 2018

MY ALWAYS ONE

Stand-one, sexy friends to lovers contemporary romance

July 2021

* * *

INDULGENCE SERIES:

UNEXPECTED

August 2018

UNCONVENTIONAL

January 2018

UNFORGETTABLE

October 2019

UNDENIABLE

August 2020

ABOUT THE AUTHOR

Aleatha Romig is a New York Times, Wall Street Journal, and USA Today bestselling author who lives in Indiana, USA. She has raised three children with her high school sweetheart and husband of over thirty years. Before she became a full-time author, she worked days as a dental hygienist and spent her nights writing. Now, when she's not imagining mind-blowing twists and turns, she likes to spend her time with her family and friends. Her other pastimes include reading and creating heroes/anti-heroes who haunt your dreams!

Aleatha impresses with her versatility in writing. She released her first novel, CONSEQUENCES, in August of 2011. CONSEQUENCES, a dark romance, became a bestselling series with five novels and two companions released from 2011 through 2015. The compelling and epic story of Anthony and Claire Rawlings has graced more than half a million e-readers. Her first stand-alone smart, sexy thriller INSIDIOUS was next. Then Aleatha released the five-novel INFIDELITY series, a romantic suspense saga, that took the reading world by storm, the final book landing on three of the top bestseller lists. She ventured into traditional publishing with Thomas and Mercer. Her books INTO THE LIGHT and AWAY FROM THE DARK were published through this mystery/thriller publisher in 2016. In the spring of 2017, Aleatha again ventured into a different genre with her first fun and sexy stand-alone romantic comedy with the USA Today bestseller PLUS ONE. She continued with ONE NIGHT and ANOTHER ONE. If you like fun, sexy, novellas that make your heart pound, try her UNCONVENTIONAL and UNEXPECTED. In 2018 Aleatha returned to her dark romance roots with WEB OF SIN.

Aleatha is a "Published Author's Network" member of the Romance Writers of America and PEN America. She is represented by Kevan Lyon of Marsal Lyon Literary Agency.

Made in the USA
Monee, IL
27 June 2022

98683963R00168